# A PANTHEON OF THIEVES

*And Other Weird Tales*

## COY HALL

*For*
*Olivia*

# CONTENTS

## ❧  I  ❧

## NIGHT OF THE RATS' NEST

*July 1918*

The sound was cosmic, trembling the cratered earth, moving in the water, echoing painfully in his bones. The concussive beat lacked the chaos of German shelling, and it penetrated more deeply.

*I'm losing my mind*, he confessed.

Optimism rather than reality spawned the confession. Insanity wasn't a place to hide. His mind was strong, firm, and clear. He slid beneath the rippling, scummy water and held his breath until his lungs ached. The crater, too, was not a place to hide. The noise reached him, filling his mind, pulsing through his fingertips.

These were titanic footsteps, crushing along a moonscape that troops had christened No Man's Land.

*One—two—one—two.*

*Crash—crump—crash—crump.*

He tapped out the rhythm in his mind. Coming nearer? Had it singled him out?

Fresh from a Lakota reservation, he was green as early

summer. Rotten luck had landed his birthday in a lottery draft, and the same luck landed him in a uniform. Now he was in France, desperately bathing in a rain-filled crater on the Marne as the flash and scuttle of bombs interrupted the night.

*You* have *lost your mind. You're washing your face and hands while men die around you.*

The footfalls neared, growing louder, more resonating. Placing his back against shifting mud, he broke the water and looked at the sky. A pall of smoke, made translucent when hissing shells ignited, erased any vision of the moon or stars.

The screams of dying men reached his hole in the earth. Before halting at the crater to bathe, he'd been part of an advance crew tasked with cutting barbed wire. Falling by the crater when the German artillery first boomed, he didn't resist the urge to crawl inside.

*I shirked my duty,* he thought. *Treason probably. Execution likely. Firing squad. I abandoned those men. They think I'm dead. They'll come looking for my corpse tonight. They'll risk their lives searching for me.*

He washed mud from his neck.

*Crash—crump—crash—crump.*

He watched the high pall, searching for the source. It had to be close. A shell screamed and whistled, smashing the earth twenty yards to his right, close enough to kill. Upturned earth nearly buried him.

Before the world went dark, he expected to see death shining, not as a hooded, robed specter, but as a massive godly form looking down, as though man constituted a nest of rats. Death would be perturbed, disgusted, frightened, just as men found rats revolting.

*Like rats, Death won't kill us until it sees us.*

The footfalls broke rhythm, slowing, halting.

He felt the presence and shadow of the cosmic titan before him, even if his mind did not understand the shape.

*This is wrath*, he thought. *This is the end of the world.*

In the moment before losing consciousness, he struggled to decide whether a full moon pierced the smoky veil enclosing the Marne, or if something terrible and great opened its eye on him, finding him in the crater.

*The audacity of the rodent*, he thought, *is to stare back into the eye.*

He sank into icy water, while earth, rock, and the rubble of shattered corpses cascaded, filling the hole.

---

### December 1919

FROM HIS CLAPBOARD home in Dakota, perched on the edge of a lumpen reservation, John Black Elk watched a cabinet open around the girth of a gray rat. Intently, the rodent emerged. Nails clacked against the plank floor. Neither sunlight nor Black Elk's presence convinced the rat to scurry for cover.

Staring, his mind drifted.

The audacity of the rodent returned his mind to the war. No creature was sadder to see trenches empty than the rats. Rodents were the true admirers of Verdun, the Somme, and the Marne. War was their fat season.

Black Elk grimaced, watching the gray rat retreat to its shelter beneath the sink. The cabinet clicked shut.

*Surveilling*, he thought, *for its brood.*

Black Elk hated two things about his time in France. First was the incessant, inexhaustible activity of rats. He and two other men had made a sport of killing trench rodents, keeping a board by the firing step, carving tally marks each morning.

In a letter, he admitted to his mother: *Nothing kills rats like when the Huns drop gas.* When he wrote that, he'd wanted to appear brave, shocking, and worldly. He couldn't say whether he had or not. The words weren't brave, shocking, or worldly now. His mother couldn't say. She was dead and buried, killed by influenza before the letter reached her door.

Courageous or not, he'd watched the effect of chlorine gas on rats from behind the safety of a breathing apparatus. The army called the ugly thing a gas mask. When poison slinked into the rat nests like phantom cats, the fat bastards issued forth with drunken minds and confused feet.

Black Elk wrote in another unread letter: *We call gas the Pied Piper for the effect it has. Ma, I don't exaggerate, one of the beasts walked from its hole on hind legs and did a little pirouette before it fell on its face. If it wasn't for men suffocating at our feet, we would've laughed until it hurt. The gas makes them dance. I'll stop short of saying I wish you could see it.*

The second thing he hated was how depressing human filth could be when it went unwashed for weeks, when dirt seeped into your skin deeper than a tattoo. While wading in mud, he was afraid to admit the price he'd pay for a simple bath.

Once, he shirked duty and left his comrades to risk an icy bath in No Man's Land.

*Why are you thinking of that?* he chided.

No matter how he tried, he couldn't shut away the memory. The titan always found a way to return. The shudder of footsteps reached him. His finger twitched. The probing eye found him in the crater, watching him like an unwelcome rat.

4

Black Elk walked to the cabinet. He opened the flimsy door and looked at the rodent. With bristled fur and a pink tail, the creature wasn't large or threatening. Light turned its eyes red. The thing froze in terror.

*If I find shit on my floor, a single pellet, I'm coming after you,* he thought. *If you poke your head one more time, I'm coming after you with poison. Go mind your children.*

The rat wrinkled its nose and turned.

*I mean it, you son of a bitch.*

The rodent scurried into the shadow of pans.

Black Elk stepped into the bedroom, the only other room in his home, and touched the blanket-turned-curtain on the window. Moving it aside, he allowed in a lance of gray winter sunlight. A rutted, muddy pathway fit for horses rather than automobiles formed the view.

A knock on his door paused another grim gauntlet of memories. He crossed rooms and answered it. His uncle, who'd taken the name Jerome since finding work with a lumber company, stood on the front step, cradling a paper bag of store-bought wine. In Lakota territory, Jerome was a highly successful man, an inspiration to boarding school youth. He had fat on his bones. He was friends with white men. And in the summer, when the roads dried, he drove a yellow automobile.

"It's New Year's Eve," Jerome said merrily.

Wind gusted around him, moving black hair over his ears. He was not a particularly handsome man. The skin along his jaws was pitted and pocked, and his mouth was loose and sloppy. He'd been married and divorced twice, and he was courting a third.

"Tomorrow's the twenties, John." He smiled in his slovenly way. "Didn't think I'd live to see 'em. Did you?"

"I didn't forget," Black Elk said congenially. He forced a smile. He opened the door wider, inviting Jerome inside.

"No time, son. Just wanted to make certain I can count on you to show up. I have a neat little toy for tonight. I don't doubt you saw one of these in France."

Black Elk's hand trembled.

"It's a radio," said Jerome. "I bought the doodad last week."

---

ALONE, Black Elk wrapped a blanket around his shoulders. The wind picked up. Gusts intensified, rattling his walls.

*There's a storm coming,* Jerome had said. *If it doesn't get any colder, we'll start the year coated in ice.*

Black Elk saw an ice storm as a child. Ice cracked trees and brought the world to a standstill just as effectively as a good shelling. There had been trees on the ground for miles, felled in a line.

God, it was difficult to find distraction in winter. He tried to read an old magazine. Then he tried to think of his mother and Jerome, whose older brother perished at Wounded Knee. Black Elk's family was involved with the Ghost Dance then, but all that had fallen away, blasted by Hotchkiss guns.

He thought about whether the pieces of his life would find order in the twenties, a new decade. He thought about children on the reservation, learning English and dollars with modern haircuts.

When he fell asleep, Black Elk dreamed of trenches, dancing rats, and a quaking in the ground brought about by massive steps rather than bombs.

---

AT DUSK, John Black Elk exited his home.

Wind brought freezing rain rather than snow to the hills. As Jerome predicted, a skin of ice left a sheen on the land. The walk to his uncle's house, which crowned a sloping hill, would be treacherous. From where he stood, he spied oil lights burning in Jerome's windows. People had arrived. The party had begun.

The single-story brick abode was the most opulent building on the reservation, providing a stark contrast with the flurry of shacks in the valley below. His uncle's home towered like a chateau above peasant shanties. Some Lakota jokingly referred to Jerome as Mayor because he knew the county sheriff personally. He was a good American.

Black Elk continued his effort at distraction. He looked forward to being too intoxicated to think.

*Maybe I'll be rebellious in the twenties*, he thought. *Be a bad influence on the children.*

He started along the path, still more mud than ice. Rain and hail pelted the tarpaulin wrapped around his head and shoulders. Mud sucked at his boots. Icy water reached his feet.

*Then again, maybe I'll take a job like Jerome, make a wage, buy a house, buy a car, a wife, turn white. Have a pocket itching to be filled with dollars, as Jerome says.*

Fewer and fewer Lakota were reticent about entering that world.

*Get in line, brother. Look at Jerome. Look at success. Look at the women on his arms. Watch that farting, burping car move, brother.*

The sight of the cemetery, a patch of earth bloated with influenza victims like his mother, a garden decorated in Christian symbols, blasted apart his musing.

*Things end so quickly*, he thought. *The world may not make it to 1920. Why plan? Tonight might be the last of it.*

Black Elk entered Jerome's home without knocking.

The warmth of a fire reached him, thawing his nerves. His face and hands gained feeling again.

Two white men sat beside each other on the couch—young, conspicuously sober, in search of Indian girls. The other guests were Lakota, people Black Elk had known his entire life, a few young, a few old. Alcohol had loosened everyone's lips, so that a mix of conversations filled the room. With a quick glance, Black Elk counted ten.

When Jerome spotted his nephew, he brought the chatter to a halt.

"The man of the hour is here," he said. He raised his hands, one gripping a wine bottle, for punctuation.

*I never agreed to this*, Black Elk thought miserably. He wanted to be home, watching the rat in the kitchen. He hated attention. He hated when eyes fell upon him. Uncomfortably, he returned the smiles of the group. He stripped the tarpaulin and set the bundle aside to dry.

Jerome sauntered forward, already drunk. Too drunk. Sloppy drunk.

"Come here, son," he said, wrapping his arm around Black Elk's shoulder, spilling wine on his nephew's clean shirt.

Black Elk frowned at the stain.

Jerome smiled. "Honey, come over here. This is more than a celebration of our engagement," he slurred. "More than another New Year. Much more."

The engagement was news to Black Elk. He watched as Jerome's soon-to-be third wife separated from the crowd. She was only a teenager—black hair to her shoulders, coal-dark eyes, a shy smile. Sheepishly, she displayed the diamond and gold on her finger.

Jerome laughed too long and loud. He wrapped his other arm around his fiancé.

"Chumani, this is my nephew, John."

Chumani nodded, color spotting her cheeks.

Black Elk pitied the girl. She didn't know what she was doing. Jerome's magnetism, his pomp and prosperity, had ensnared her. He would use her up.

"John, this is a lot to ask, son. We got a crystal radio set rigged in the kitchen, and we got Chumani, who is a medium—you know what a medium does—and we got you, who fought in the war and, I'd say, has seen more dead than all of us put together."

"I—"

"—Hold that thought and hear me out, son. Now I got two dopes here that think the world will end tonight. Amen?" Jerome eyed the white men on the couch. "What'd you call yourselves?"

In unison, the men took drinks rather than offer rebuttal.

"Spiritualists," one grumbled. "And we never said—"

"So, in light of that possibility, we're gonna celebrate the New Year by getting in contact with the other side. Right, honey?" Jerome released Black Elk and hugged his fiancé. He kissed her forehead.

Black Elk, more confused than angry, asked, "What in the hell do I have to do with it?"

Jerome lowered his voice beneath the resuming chatter. "Chumani believes…." His mind stalled. "Honey, tell him what you believe."

The girl spoke with confidence. "When a man sees Death, a piece of Death's spirit gets inside him. A man that sees war lives with one foot in the grave."

*She's Sioux*, Black Elk thought, *and armed with proverbs.*

He wondered if he'd lash out at the girl if she were old and ugly. Did beauty still his temper? Maybe it was less her prettiness and more her sincerity. Regardless, he spoke his mind, albeit calmly.

"That's a load of shit," he said.

"You're a conduit," Chumani countered, undaunted.

"Why the radio?" Black Elk had experience with radio communication—it was part of his military training.

"Chumani says the dead float around you like dust in sunlight. They travel in the.... What's it called, honey?"

"The ether," Chumani said. "Like radio waves."

"They travel in the ether," Jerome said. "Radio's like a telephone."

Black Elk watched Chumani's eyes, wondering who manipulated whom in the relationship.

"Where's the wine?" he asked. "I want to be drunk first."

Jerome handed over his bottle.

"You won't be able to buy that in a store come January," he said. "Prohibition's enough to end the world, isn't it? That's Biblical. Amen?"

His gaze found the white men on the couch.

They were listening.

Jerome threw his head back and guffawed.

———

*ABOVE ALL, the rats were thieves.*

*"Just take a look inside that nest," Baker, a man who later met with a splinter of shrapnel, who drowned in blood, said.*

*In addition to tufts of cloth and a smattering of mess tins, Black Elk spotted rifle shell casings in the pilfered bounty.*

*"Blind greed," Baker explained.*

*"They're not smart. Maybe they tried to eat them," Black Elk offered.*

*Why did he feel the need to defend these obnoxious creatures? Was he not one of their executioners?*

*"I wish they were more inclined to eat bullets. I'd feed 'em a*

*few." Bravely, Baker lit a cigarette. The orange tip was a prime target for snipers.*

*"I guess I'm sentimental tonight. I pity the bastards."*

*Baker shook his head. "You're touched, chap. Touched up here."*

*"Seems more fair when we hunt them. They can't hide from gas. There's no sport."*

*"You should cut up your coat and make them tiny masks. You won't lose the sport that way."*

One of the spiritualists offered a glass of whiskey. The man's closeness, and the stink of liquor on his breath, stole Black Elk from the memory.

"Who are you?" Black Elk asked. Before the man answered, he added, "I thought the world was ending once. I was convinced."

*Why are you talking?* It was either liquid courage or stupidity. His consciousness funneled downward.

"My name's Baker," the man said.

"Baker?" Black Elk shook his head.

*You're dead*, he thought. *Shrapnel cut through an artery in your arm. You bled out. I was there.*

The man nodded. "I know Chumani through one of our local groups."

"I thought you worked with Jerome. I thought you were trying to fuck our women."

Baker shook his head, nonplussed. "Chumani has immense talent, you know. And I think she's right about you, about your experiences." After a pause, "What'd you say about the world ending?"

Black Elk gulped the whiskey. He coughed and grimaced, wondering how much liquor he'd have to mix with wine to become violently ill. He considered telling the story of the cosmic being he'd been witness to, but he refrained. He wasn't drunk enough to revisit the memory, or to talk to strangers about destructive gods and fragile men. As the words remained dammed, he thought again of the moon-like eye.

"Listen to that ice," Jerome said, entering the living room. "It's bringing down trees." He raised his voice. "Alright, everybody, into the kitchen. We got it set up. We're ready."

"Can I tell you about my thoughts on the world, Baker?" Black Elk asked. Maybe it was less the alcohol and more the possibility he spoke to a man long dead.

"Please do."

"We're all rats. And there are bigger things that find us nosey and obnoxious."

"Skewed and odd, I'd say, chap."

"Chap?"

*Baker was British. He said things like chap. What happened to your accent, Baker? Did you lose it in the ether?*

"Come on, let's go to the kitchen."

Black Elk felt like he was outside his body.

"This," he said, waving his hand, "is our nest. Chumani is about to poke her head out of the hole. Me, too, Baker. We used to dangle pieces of bread on a string to get rats to poke out their heads. Then you know what happened?"

"No."

*Yes, you do.*

"They'd do it. They never learned. We'd... *blam*. We shot them. You know, I never thought of it, but that wasn't much sport either, was it? That was dirty."

"Come on, soldier. I think you need to set the liquor aside." Baker reached out and slid his hand around Black Elk's arm.

In the kitchen, Jerome stood by the dining table with his contraption, a crystal radio set, at his hip. The device was a simple construction: a series of copper wires wrapped around a cylinder, metal clips, a metal box, two long wires with earphones, all atop a board.

Chumani took a seat when everyone entered. With her elbows on the table, she faced the radio.

"John, you're a little green. Are you okay?"

Black Elk moved to the radio. "I don't know how to use one of these," he admitted. "Not one this primitive."

Jerome leaned to his ear. "Why don't you slow down on the wine, huh? Looks like your eyes are in another universe, son."

*I don't feel drunk*, Black Elk thought. *I feel like I'm back in a crater on the Marne.* He remembered the icy water, how soothing it was when the broth soaked his crusted uniform.

"No need for you to work anything. Your job is simply to listen. Chumani's pal here...." He snapped his fingers. "What's your name, son?"

The other white man stood at Chumani's shoulder. "Thompson," he said distractedly. He bent and whispered to Chumani.

*Thompson died, too,* Black Elk thought. *He was the Lieutenant in our unit. Remember? He talked to you about his wife. He poked his head above the trench wall and a sniper blew off the back of his skull. As he was carted off, we covered blood and brain with shovelfuls of earth. Remember? You thought about writing a letter to Thompson's wife. You never did. Shame on you. You never did. Why not?*

Black Elk approached the man. "Do I know you?" he asked.

"No, I'm afraid you don't."

"I did know you, though, didn't I, Thompson? At the Marne?"

"Please, we need to concentrate."

Jerome touched Black Elk's shoulder. "Why don't you

go ahead and have a seat, son? You're making people uncomfortable."

Black Elk, confused, moved to the other side of the table. He sat. The crowd—it had grown larger—gathered around Jerome. It felt as though everyone on the reservation entered the room, expanding the walls, huddling against the storm. Black Elk lost count of the faces. There were at least twenty. Additional white men stood in the back, pressed against the sink. He only saw down to their collars, but they wore uniforms.

"Mr. Thompson here," Jerome continued, "will be our engineer for the evening."

*Where's Baker?* Black Elk thought. *Hadn't he pushed me in here in the first place?* He wasn't among the faces. *Maybe he left. I disturbed him—seeing him like that, seeing him for who he really is, a man who died 4000 miles away. I'll get to Thompson, too. He knows I know. He'll get up into the ether and go away, just like his buddy. Who are they to cheat death? To return?*

*Who are you to cheat death?*

"Chumani, dear, I'll step aside, and you can tell them what you will." Jerome, smiling, was having the time of his life. He made no effort to conceal his excitement.

Chumani put her hands flat against the table.

*Chumani means dew drops*, Black Elk thought. *Fitting name for a pretty girl.*

The thought set in Black Elk's mind, the normality of it reaching into other areas of his imagination.

*You're okay*, another voice said. *You're gonna be fine. Can you hear me?*

The voice belonged to York, a Minnesotan who rescued him from his cavity in the earth when the *crump* of mortars and explosion of shells ceased. York pulled him from the rubble, exhumed him.

*You don't have a scratch, John, you lucky bastard.*

*I saw something,* Black Elk said hysterically. *I saw the God of Death. He looked down on me. He opened his eye. I hid from him. I went down into the water, hiding from him.*

*Rest, buddy. You just close your eyes and rest. Your brain's rattled.*

"Mr. Black Elk," Chumani said, "I'd like you to put one of the earphones to your ear. Pick it up, please."

Black Elk nodded. He pressed the ceramic piece against his ear.

"Mr. Thompson will take the other. Mr. Thompson, will you explain?"

"Gladly." Straightening his back, the white man addressed the crowd. "Our society is committed to utilizing technology to speak with those deceased. We believe that radio can reach, can single out voices as they traverse the ether."

"Oh, stifle it, Thompson," Jerome said. "World's gonna end before you finish your spiel. Amen?"

"I have never said 'amen' in that context. I don't understand why you insist upon making that insipid joke."

Jerome slapped his knee and laughed. After he caught his breath, he said, "Get on with the show, honey. Forget the egghead talk."

A crash with the resonance of thunder caught the crowd unaware, and everyone stopped to listen. Ice had built in layers over the ground, homes, and trees, growing heavy and destructive. Murmurs of anxiety passed through the assembly.

"Damn, there goes another tree," Jerome said. "That one was close."

*That wasn't a tree*, Black Elk thought, and his spine froze in recognition. *I've heard that sound before.*

A second thunderous boom trembled the table and radio apparatus.

*The rhythm of footsteps,* Black Elk thought. Fear surfaced in his throat with the tang of copper.

*You're okay. You're gonna be fine.*

A smattering of Lakota words caught his attention. He looked across at Chumani, who, with Thompson hovering at her shoulder, chanted. Given his cue, Thompson fiddled with the radio. A burst of white noise entered Black Elk's ear.

"I hear them," Chumani said. "Very busy. The veil is thin."

The crowd tightened.

"Give me the other earpiece," Jerome said, grabbing the wire from Thompson.

*One—two—one—two.*

Outside, something large pressed the forest to the ground with rhythmic precision.

A voice, couched in static, emerged.

Jerome's eyes widened.

"What is it?" someone asked.

"You'll get your turn," Jerome said.

Chumani looked at Black Elk. "What do *you* hear?" she asked.

"Squealing rats," he said.

"That ain't what I heard, you nut," Jerome said. "I—"

"—Quiet. He is our conduit. Let him interpret. Go on," Chumani said, gentle as a coaxing mother.

Black Elk shut his eyes and allowed static to enter his mind. He tried to untangle intermittent breaks in the fuzz. The static, just like the cold crater water on the Marne, concealed him, afforded him a chance to hide. With concentration, the squeal of rats became a mix of high voices.

"Snippets of words," he said.

Thompson looked at Chumani. "You were right," he said. "He's pulling them in in droves."

Chumani frowned. "Find one of the voices and concentrate."

She took the earpiece from Jerome. Reaching across the table, she beckoned Black Elk. He brought his trembling hand to her fingertips. With her touch, the individual voices grew more distinct. Chumani resumed her chant, a whisper over her parted lips.

*Crash—crump—crash—crump.*

"It's pressing down trees like wheat stalks," Black Elk said.

"Concentrate."

"It's coming for us."

"Please, Mr. Black Elk, focus."

He teased a thin voice from the chaotic chatter.

*God,* he thought, *it's York again.*

Indeed, the Minnesotan who'd been shot in the mouth, emerged from the ether's cacophony.

*This time,* York said, *I can't help you, John.*

*Why?* Black Elk thought. *What happened to you?*

*You should've stayed in your nest, John. Listen. It's not only outside. It's in here, too. Do you hear it?*

*Crash-crump-crash-crump.*

The cosmic footsteps, inside the wires, dissipated static like wind through fog. Suddenly, in their wake, the radio was clear and silent, an absolute hush. For the first time, he heard more than the titan's approach.

Chumani's eyes grew wide.

Black Elk discarded the ceramic earpiece, and it clattered across the table.

"What is it?" Jerome asked. "What happened?"

Black Elk threw back his chair and pushed into the crowd. He kept his eyes from their faces. He did not want to see the men with whom he served, soldiers who crumpled beneath the step of Death. He passed to the living room, and then to the front door, as Jerome called out behind him.

"John, son, it's okay! What happened? Chumani, what happened?"

Black Elk stepped into the frosty night. In the moonlight, the world was crystal-coated, glinting and twinkling. Treetops hung to the ground with shattered-bone limbs. Black Elk tried to run but fell hard on his hip. Pain lanced through his body, but it wasn't enough to stop him. He had to get away from the house. What if the titan came when the others surrounded him? Would they not be crushed, too? Gaining his feet, he shuffled along the icy path with all the haste he could manage. He fell again. He rose again.

Jerome was shouting out the door when Black Elk started down the hill. Chumani, a shadow against firelight, stood at his side.

Death approached from the forest. Not only did he hear it, he felt the oppression of its shadow. The ice under his feet was alive with the vibrations of the titan's advance.

The sight of the hillside graveyard stopped him. Tonight, with ice glazing its stones and crystallizing the grass, it was one of the most beautiful sights he'd ever seen. The storm had passed, leaving the moon to shine over the land like candlelight in a cave of gems.

*I'll give up here*, Black Elk thought. *Where better to end the chase?*

*Crash—crump—crash—crump.*

He shuffled toward a line of graves, each dated 1918. Here the young and old rested, his mother among them, victims not of bullets but flu germs. He knelt and ran his hand across the icy coating on a stone cross. The freeze bit his fingers. He wondered if his mother had been as intimately aware of Death, if she, like her son, cowered beneath its footsteps.

"Once," he whispered to the ground, "I thought it was bringing the word to an end. It seemed too large and cumbersome for one life. I was wrong," he said. "I poked my head into the ether and Death told me so. Death had been looking for me. I'd been hiding."

*Crash—crump—crash—crump.*

An enormous tree branch came down against the stones at the rear of the cemetery. The forest parted.

*It's here,* he thought. *I wonder if I'll go haunting like Baker, Thompson, and York, a-haunting in search of rats.*

Atop the hill, in a home that appeared indestructible to most on the reservation, a few bricks rattled from their mortar. Chuman, with her face against a frosted window-pane, shrieked.

Above the cemetery, high in the air, the eye opened again.

# THE SHE-WOLF AND SAINT EDMUND

A wolf snout, lined with black gums and ending in a curious nose, appeared in the gap of the doorway. A paw touched the hardpack floor. When the frame trembled, the door creaked inward.

Fitzgibbon peered across the room at the intruder, and he knew he wasn't dreaming. Since morning, he'd heard wolves, an entire society of them, searching, scavenging, rending, mating, and feeding. The wolves engorged themselves and vomited, and then engorged themselves again. In the village—a church steeple surrounded by hovels in a burned out clearing—there was an enormous amount of feeding to be done.

Plague had entered the settlement on the breath of a Dutch traveler, and within a month the village was decimated. The Black Death worked quickly and viciously. Of the dead, only the first coterie lay buried in the cemetery. The remainder turned homes into tombs, where carcasses lay rotting, clutching possessions, clutching one another, or clutching the nearest surface with claw-like grips. Limbs blackened. Moss sprouted between tell-tale boils on their hides. Mouths were agape, while flies copulated in their throats, and maggots writhed.

The miasma beckoned wolves, but wolves are cautious creatures. The predators did not bluster in at the first sign of weakness. Patiently, the animals waited for plague to complete its work. A pack had ringed the village, waiting days for the right moment to enter. Only this morning, before light, did the wolves spread into thoroughfares and passageways like cargo rats loosed on a dock, following their bellies.

Until now, the wolves had spared Fitzgibbon's home. Either the pack waited for him to die, he reasoned, or the animals postponed a fight until they were satiated on fallen fruit.

With a subtle grind of resistance, the door opened fully. The sky was the color of fire. Leaves fell copiously. The wolf that crossed his threshold was unwary. The mouth curled, revealing blood-stained fangs pinioned with sinew.

*A she-wolf*, Fitzgibbon thought.

Her nostrils flared, catching the infested scent of Fitzgibbon's wife and children shriveled in the corner. She bristled with excitement. The banded fur of white and gray over her withers was heavy as a mane. Her pregnant stomach bulged. Her eyes were dark like coal, and crimson speckled her nose.

Nothing the she-wolf could do equaled the pain of boils pocking Fitzgibbon's armpits and neck, or the blood drowning his lungs, or the sores that opened from lying in corrosive piss. Fitzgibbon bared his teeth, a gesture that matched the wolf.

The she-wolf inched closer. She didn't take the stance of a predator. She stood so near that Fitzgibbon smelled carrion on her warm breath. She was puzzled that the man yet lived.

In that moment, Fitzgibbon's mind broke free, like muscle detached from bone. Lying in his home, surrounded by corpses and ghosts, and faced with a curious wolf, what else could be expected? The thought entered like a dream and held sway. When the detachment remained, any absurdity gained currency.

It was then that the wolf spoke.

"You are safe," she said.

Fitzgibbon shut his fevered eyes. When he opened them again, either seconds or hours later, three additional wolves stood inside his home.

The she-wolf said, "You are Saint Edmund. You are safe."

"He," Fitzgibbon managed to say, "I am not. Wolf, you're mistaken. The shrine of Saint Edmund is near, but I am not he."

Unmoved, the she-wolf continued.

"A wolf protected you, Saint Edmund. Do you not remember? I protected you." She rose taller with pride. Her chest swelled "God bade me protect you."

With a broken effort, Fitzgibbon told the wolf that he did not remember this and that his name was not Edmund, nor was he a saint. He knew little of the Saint Edmund legend, but even children in East Anglia knew that Danes severed the old king's head. Rhymes preserved the tale. A she-wolf, enchanted by God, protected the martyred head from destruction. This was in Saxon days.

"Are you the she-wolf that protected the king?" Fitzgibbon asked.

The wolf inched closer. Rot slicked her tongue. Her eyes were pools without feeling. The mouth did not move when she spoke. Her voice bloomed in his mind.

"I'll protect you again, Saint Edmund," she said. "I'll lead you from the forest."

Fever made men mad. He'd seen the transformation with his brother-in-law.

*What does it matter then*, Fitzgibbon thought, *if we converse, she and I?*

"Is that a promise?" he asked. On the brink of death, he did not need her word, but he desired it. With time so short, guarantees, even if meaningless, were prudent.

"I'll protect you," she said.

"From what?" Fitzgibbon blathered. If he had the strength to laugh, he would have cackled. "From your friends?"

"Come, Saint Edmund," the she-wolf said. She creased her jaws and bit at cloth covering Fitzgibbon's chest. The material, thin as gauze, ripped when she pulled.

"Stand up," she ordered. The dilemma puzzled her.

"I'm too weak," Fitzgibbon said.

He looked toward the stygian shapes of his wife and children in the corner. He would have given anything to possess the strength to shove their bodies out the door.

"Like them, I'm dying. Pestilence," he said. "Plague."

The she-wolf was not stumped for long. An idea seized her, and she walked to the foot of the bed. She took Fitzgibbon's ankle into her great jaws, and then she pulled. Illness made the man light as straw, so she yanked him from the mat with one great thrust. He slammed against the floor, smashing a boil, and his mind went red with agony. The she-wolf shook his leg like a trophy. Fitzgibbon gasped, and the image was that of a skull with a broken jawbone. He gasped, but he didn't have the strength to scream.

The she-wolf pulled Fitzgibbon into the evening air. Decay and moss perfumed the village, and yet it was freeing to be out of the cloying hovel. Mud, shit, leaves, and discarded bones lined the paths. Over this, she dragged Fitzgibbon, while other wolves ransacked his home, rending the corpses inside. Fitzgibbon watched the church pass as he neared the forest's edge.

"Where are we going?" he asked.

"I'll take you to Him," the she-wolf said.

"How is it that you speak my language?" he asked. "It's uncommon for a wolf."

"How do you speak mine?" she countered. "It's God's work. You shall see. I will take you to Him."

Fitzgibbon conceded the point.

*Indeed*, he thought. *She knows God—has a long relationship with Him. Many hundreds of years.*

When the she-wolf stopped, she stood panting over Fitzgibbon. He watched her, uncertain. He was not so light that he didn't trouble her pregnant frame. She was exhausted. Another wolf, even larger than she, a mate that was traveling along at a cautious distance, sauntered across the clearing. His padded footfalls were noiseless. Another gray, he nodded at the she-wolf. She took Fitzgibbon's ankle, from which she'd torn the skin, into her mouth. Her mate bit the other ankle, his teeth grinding bone. The power in his jaws was immediately apparent. Blood poured in rivulets to Fitzgibbon's groin.

Together, the wolves marched backwards, dragging their quarry through bramble and briar.

After a distance, Fitzgibbon said, "He doesn't speak?"

Through grinding teeth, the she-wolf confirmed that her mate did not speak, not in a manner Fitzgibbon could appreciate.

The journey continued. Roots ripped and stones bruised Fitzgibbon's mottled back. He didn't know how far he'd traveled, but it was night when he and the wolves arrived at their destination. Having gone ahead, other wolves were there, waiting and pacing. All the wolves were healthy and fat—such was the bounty of plague years. The young were robust, the old fortified.

A circle tightened around the she-wolf, her mate, and the delirious Fitzgibbon. The wolves dropped his feet against the earth. His limbs were numb, so he felt nothing. There were stars in the sky, great dashes of them visible through the trees.

The she-wolf neared.

"It is God, Saint Edmund," she said. "As promised."

At first, he thought she meant the moon, but this was incorrect. When she gestured with her muzzle, Fitzgibbon craned his neck to see. God was a dark shape beneath the branches of an ancient yew. Breath emerged from the shape in clouds of frost.

Proudly, the she-wolf sat on her haunches.

"We brought him to you," she told God. "In the land of the dead, Saint Edmund alone lived."

God stepped forward, parting the wolves like a lord. God walked on hind legs, Fitzgibbon observed, but the legs did not take the shape of a man's legs. The legs were crooked, bent backwards at the knees. The gait was discordant. The figure was tall and slender above shaggy hips. Darkness masked the lines of His face, but there was something human in the configuration: two eyes, a wide mouth, hair like sprouts of laurel. God smelled like woodsmoke and rotten meat.

"She thinks I'm Saint Edmund," Fitzgibbon said.

God shrugged. Fur bristled on His shoulders. Frost emerged from the enormous mouth.

"She said that you are God."

"No," God muttered. "The she-wolf is insane. She's very old. She says many things that are untrue." The voice was not abhorrent. And, unlike the wolf's, the voice moved in the air.

"What do you want with me?" Fitzgibbon asked.

A force inside him withered. He looked at the she-wolf for protection, but she was admiring God.

God brushed aside the question. "There was only one left?" He asked the she-wolf.

Her snout dipped in shame. "Only one," she said.

God shook His head in disappointment.

"Move quicker with the next village," He said to the assembled wolves. Then, to the she-wolf, "Open him. I'll eat him raw."

The she-wolf obeyed. Her mate joined in the scissoring.

As Fitzgibbon surmised, fear did not translate to mobility, nor thought to action. He was too close to death to fight back, so near that his limbs were hardened, useless. He gasped when his skin opened, and, this time, Fitzgibbon screamed—a noise the forest ate.

## ✣ 3 ✣

## HOUE OF THE CAT'S EYE

The woman uttered a word that, to villagers in Brandenburg, was a repugnant curse. "*Landsknecht*," she said, which meant mercenary. She paused, and the noises around her—scraping armor, the din of a wagon, birds in the trees, horses—became clearer. Met with no objections, the woman continued praying in a pidgin of German and Latin.

*Landsknecht* pulled Tristram from a delirious fugue. Opening his eyes a moment of clarity blessed him. To his puzzlement, he was on his back, stripped of breastplate and buff coat, riding in an open cart. Sunlight and shade, sunlight and shade: sensations as the cart passed beneath tree canopies. His arms and legs were heavy as stone.

In a hasty withdrawal, Lieutenant Groza must have counted Tristram among the dead. He had, he presumed, been lifted from the battlefield by scavengers. Opportunistic war rats flourished in devastated regions of the empire.

The woman, who clutched a wooden cross, ceased her prayer and watched Tristram. Lines of worry formed at

29

the corners of her mouth. She turned and looked at someone Tristram could not see.

A man's voice then, in German of the lower sort: "He's weak as a foundling," he said. "Look at his leg. What can he do to you?"

Tristram did not protest. He doubted he had strength to speak, let alone lift his hand against a villager. He'd lost too much blood to be a threat to anyone. Groza was wise to leave him for dead. He looked the part. He recalled the initial shock of the wound, the sound of it, and he marveled that he'd survived this long.

"*Landsknecht*," the woman hissed. With disdain, she looked in Tristram's eyes.

Before fading, Tristram took in another sight. The cart was fairly empty, returning from a journey rather than embarking. A heap of armor (his blade and harquebus were nowhere in sight) lay in one corner, while a pile of wooden figurines filled the other. Except passengers, this was the only cargo. Tristram concentrated, which was imprudent with little strength, to make out details of the carvings.

He looked upon a hoard of wooden cats—toys to hock at a fair, but with the fine work of delicate faces and eyes. One of the cats looked back at him with the trailing eyes of a portrait. He matched the stare. The cat squinted. *Delirium*.

The woman began her prayer anew. It occurred to Tristram that the words interspersed with German were not Latin but a tongue he couldn't decipher. She seemed to be invoking names.

*A prayer for what?* Tristram wondered, because it was surely not for his recovery, not when peppered with vitriol. A few blistered, incoherent thoughts came between him and unconsciousness, a shock of agony erupted in his crushed leg, and then all was mercifully dark.

---

IT WAS night when Tristram awoke. Rather than the splintered planks of the cart, gentle straw prodded his back. For a moment, the stillness was peaceful, the darkness calming. There were no candles around, but a window allowed moonlight into the room. A breeze, too, entered, cooling sweat on his face. It was summer and the night was warm. Wood smoke irritated his swollen throat. He wondered if discomfort woke him.

*No*, he realized quickly. *It's the leg.*

He slowed his rapid breathing. He felt as though a torch prodded muscle and bone. The agony was maddening. Nausea curdled his stomach.

In a testament of will, he gathered himself to look about the room. The sight of anything would be grounding. He tilted his neck, careful not to see the leg, and he peered at the walls. A figure near the window, silvered by moonlight, caught him by surprise. He had thought himself alone. The shape, that of a man, sat on a ledge protruding from the wall. The man clutched the edge and tilted forward. He was either so high or so short that his legs dangled without touching the floor. Shadow obscured his face.

Tristram greeted the man inelegantly. A simple *"Who's there?"*, graveled by pain, escaped him.

A beat of silence followed. The figure offered no response. It remained still.

Tristram became aware of similar figures that ringed the room in which he lay. A ledge extended around the wall, interrupted by the window and an open doorway. He did not possess the strength to rise and look behind him, but from the continuity of shapes he saw, he assumed these men filled every space of the bench. It was like a clandestine tribunal. Or watchmen noosing their quarry.

Nothing moved. Despite his effort, he could not make out faces.

Tristram remembered the feline statues in the cart.

*Carvings*, he thought, amazed.

He returned to the first figure, perched at the window and swaddled with more light than the others. He denied his unease, imagining the skill it required to do such work, but movement in the silvered man obliterated his effort at calmness.

The knuckled joints of the hand creaked, gripping, and the wooden man leaned forward. It was a subtle but perceptible alteration, enough to bring the head into moonlight, like bas-relief from shadow.

Whereas the cat possessed lifelike eyes, this figure had no eyes at all. Rather, a mask of crisscrossed limbs and vines caged the head. With masked face in view, the figure stopped moving. The hands loosened and relaxed.

For several beats, Tristram watched and waited. His heart was fast, and the rush of blood weakened him.

Footsteps.

In terror, as light spread into the room, he looked to the doorway. The woman who had prayed over him in the cart stood there, framed in the soft glow of a candle, puzzled. Her face was imprinted on his fevered mind. He recognized her at once. The flame trembled in her grip.

"Did you speak?" she asked. Her voice, too, lived in his mind.

Tristram reclined his head, relieved that she had come. He nodded.

The woman brought the candle forward, and light

touched the wooden statues. Each carving had jointed arms, legs, and hands, and each wore a mask of limb and vine. Figures lined the walls like marionettes in the shop of a puppeteer, but these were not toys. He wondered if they were funeral effigies. He had seen such work, complete with garments and plaster death masks, in the funeral processions of the rich. Tristram's father kept such an effigy as an eternal guardian in his tomb. It was a common practice, but he'd never encountered the craftsmen of such things.

The woman stood at his side. There was something Gaelic in her appearance, ancestry that belied her accent and home in Brandenburg. Her hair was auburn and her skin pale, touched with freckles across a delicate nose. Her eyes, too, were pale.

"You are not German," she said. "What language were you speaking? Dutch?"

"English," Tristram said in German that had become precise from two years fighting in the Catholic League. "I come from Scotland."

She stood out of arm's reach. Scotland meant little to her. It was a world away.

"In your prayer," Tristram said, "you also spoke another tongue. Was it Latin?"

"No," she said. "Much older than Roman words." She extended the flame and looked into his eyes. After a moment, she said, "You're frightened. Why?"

"Where should I begin?" he started. He approximated a smile, which, coupled with his death's head pallor and slovenly beard, was ghastly.

The woman did not find him amusing. She waited.

"One of the figures moved," he admitted, and then, less secure in his assertion, "or so it appeared in the dark."

The woman's grin was inadvertent, telling.

"The one by the window," he said, eager to have his fears dashed.

She stepped toward the shelf. The carvings were not as large as they had been before. The one by the window was little more than four feet tall. The ledge was not high.

"This one?" she asked, amused.

*Or pleased*, he wondered. Although he didn't want it to be there, he detected a touch of cruelty.

"Don't ridicule a fevered mind," Tristram said.

"This one here?" She pushed the wooden man back into place, pressing its head against the wall. The joints creaked. "Did he lean forward?"

"So it seemed," Tristram said.

"Ah, but the wind will do that. God forbid a gust drop him to the ground." She laughed, and it was a nice laugh despite the intention, pleasing as a windchime. "What's your name, *landsknecht*? You carried no papers. And the ranting you do in your sleep is mad."

"Tristram Carew," he said. He wondered what other information he divulged in sleep. He omitted that he fought for Groza and the Catholics. He did not, despite her correct assumption, admit his status as a mercenary. "What's yours?"

"Liliana," she said. She thought a moment. "Tristram is a knight's name. A knight's name for a *landsknecht* is quite funny. Did you give yourself the name? Is it good for business?"

Tristram was too weak to counter the ribbing. His father, a martial soul, named him after a figure of Arthurian romance. Tristram's brother was Percival Carew. He was impressed she knew of Arthur. He offered the ghastly smile again.

"How is your leg feeling?" Liliana asked with less levity.

Her face, in shadows thrown by candlelight, grew appropriately grave.

*You're dangerously bright*, he thought. Maybe it was a fever dream but, like a sudden burst of color in his mind, he intuited, *You're a wonderful imitation of life, Liliana. You perform the role very well. You could make someone love, hate, admire, or fear you, or you could make all those things true at once.* Watching her left Tristram in Purgatory.

When Tristram did not respond, Liliana fetched him a ladle of water. He drank greedily, and the liquid ignited pain in his throat. He drank another ladleful before admitting he did not possess the courage to look at his leg, and he hadn't since the moment it was crushed.

With sympathy, Liliana said, "Gird yourself and look." She hovered the candle over the end of his straw mattress. The light reached his neck. She lifted the blanket. "It saved your life," she said.

Tristram found the courage to look. As he did, he cried, unrestrained like a child. His right leg was severed above the knee. The wound was cauterized. Infection discolored the rawness.

Liliana sat on the floor at his side.

"Be calm," she said. "Be calm. You would not have lived. Before this, the infection was worse. Your foot was rotten."

He grabbed her hand, and she allowed him to hold on for comfort. She prayed for him, mixing in the unfamiliar tongue, and he went unconscious beneath her lilting voice.

---

"HE AIN'T likely to walk on a crutch, is he?" one man said to the other. The accent was rural, the voice lazily bellicose. "Leg's gettin' rotted again."

The other man shrugged. "Smells that way. Fetch a vegetable cart," he ordered someone unseen, someone standing outside the window. "He's weak as a foundling. I doubt he'll stay awake long enough to walk."

The first man, young with a red peasant face, knelt at Tristram's side. The smell of manure was heavy on his clothes, ratty save for an ill-fitting leather jerkin. Tristram wondered if that garment, too, was salvaged from the battlefield. Ungrateful though the feeling was, a spark of anger made him more aware. He rose to his elbow, signaling strength. He wondered if the villagers were war rats—desperate night-men who descended on battlefields and pillaged the dead. War rats were ghoulish scum.

The other man, older but equally undistinguished and poorly bred, stood near the window. It was afternoon and the sun was high. His voice, like Liliana's, was familiar.

"Gotta move you from the workshop," he told Tristram. "I'm certain you won't find the trip agreeable, but we'll cart you rather than have you hop."

Tristram nodded uncertainly.

*A workshop*, he thought.

In the light of day, he saw that the figures lining the room were, indeed, funeral effigies. Off putting, certainly, but lacking magic. Masks protected the smooth surface of wood until plaster faces could be applied. The faces would be death masks of the deceased. A menagerie of animals waited on a shelf above the human figures: cats, foxes, bears, rabbits, stags, and horses.

The heavy youth, noticing Tristram's interest in the carvings, said, "He saw one of the little men move, he did." He laughed until his body heaved. There was something off about the man, something infantile. Great turbulence waited, barely restrained, behind his eyes. All he needed was a reason for violence.

The older man did not laugh. He stepped forward.

"Moving will hurt," he cautioned. "Nothin' you aren't used to, but it'll hurt all the same." From his coat, he drew a hank of leather. He handed it to Tristram. "Best bite down on that," he said with sympathy. "My name's Ambrus. The lad there slobbering on you is Rowland."

Tristram offered his name and then clenched the leather between his teeth.

Ambrus nodded. "At least you're not talkin' nonsense now. Maybe your fever will lighten."

Ambrus and Rowland lifted Tristram from the ground. The jostling of the severed limb brought cold sweat to his brow. A wave of nausea passed through him. The agony was consuming. Splotches of color glossed his eyes. He wavered and came close to succumbing.

"You gonna be sick?" Ambrus asked.

Tightly, Tristram shook his head. The focus made him sicker.

"Quickly," Ambrus ordered Rowland.

The men carried him from the workshop into the adjoining room. The space was small and tightly packed, living quarters with a hearth and workbenches and tools and cords of oak. There was a cramped loft with personal belongings, and at least one bed of rope and straw. The space reeked of smoke and sulfur. Ambrus and Rowland hurried out the door. Another young man, thin as his bones allowed, stood beside a vegetable cart that had two wheels and a pair of handles. He did not speak. Like a child, he sprinted off when his duty was complete.

"Bite down hard," Ambrus cautioned.

With little delicacy, he and Rowland deposited Tristram in the cart. Tristram shifted into place, trying to hide pain on his gaunt face. His left leg hung over the wall, while the sawed-off nub remained on the floor. The bone ached, and he felt a phantom pain where the crushed limb had been. He breathed. He prayed and bit the leather. His fever was not easing, as Ambrus suggested, but worsening.

"We've something to show you," Ambrus said.

In the full light of day, his advanced age was apparent. His hair, protruding from a thinly brimmed capotain, was a dirty gray. He wore a mustache of the same shade, large enough to hide his upper lip, of which a scar marred the symmetry. Deep lines crossed his brow and underscored his eyes. He looked about, ready to bark an order, but his companions had gone.

To Tristram, he muttered, "Both those boys are touched in the head."

Tristram had noticed, at least with Rowland, but he responded as if this were news.

Then, more darkly, Ambrus confided, "A *landsknecht* gave 'em a beatin' when they was boys. He beat their heads in. Just awful. He left 'em for dead. You could beat on Rowland all day, but it wouldn't do anything but bloody him. The other, Kaspar, he hasn't said a word since. That happened in Magdeburg."

Tristram stirred uneasily beneath Ambrus' glare. One never mentioned Magdeburg lightly.

"You there when they burned Magdeburg?" he asked. Ambrus grew distant, and his eyes wandered. His tone was better suited for discussing weather.

"I wasn't," Tristram said. Magdeburg had burned twelve years prior in 1631. He had not fought with the League then. "Were you?"

Ambrus nodded. He paused, allowing that to sink in, as if to say, *I know what was done. I saw.* After a moment, he said, "Here comes Rowland."

Tristram craned his neck and looked back toward the squat cottage and workshop. Rowland strode forward, belligerent, wearing Tristram's breastplate. His stomach and chest protruded on both sides of the metal, dwarfing the armor. Worse still, he wore Tristram's helmet, an heirloom forged by his father. The helmet fit Rowland so poorly that it failed to reach his ears by the width of two fingers. For amusement, he'd ripped out the helmet's plume of egret feathers. Tristram's father had brought those feathers from North Africa. Their value was sentimental. The breastplate was also damaged. Rowland had beaten large dints into it with a hammer. He gripped a hammer now.

"Humor him," Ambrus whispered. "He'll go off and play and leave us be."

Tristram lowered his eyes in shame, feeling half a man. Rowland approached, stomping over a path of stones.

*What would Groza think of you?* Tristram thought miserably. *Or your father. He not only forged that helmet, he trained you to fight and live how you lived. What would he say?*

*That you were better dead.*

*I should've died,* he thought. *I should have died that day.* His resentment grew.

When Rowland neared, he laughed grotesquely, sharing spittle. "Maybe I'll treat you like you treated me," he said, flaunting the hammer. "You're the boy now. What do you think, father?" he asked Ambrus. "You think maybe I should?"

Calmly, Ambrus shook his head. "Go now," he ordered.

Rowland looked at Tristram. His eyes were nothing but hatred. In a quieter, more level tone, he said, "Maybe I will." He lifted the hammer.

Tristram stared at his hands. A week prior he would've killed Rowland without thought. He would've opened his gut with a dagger. Then Rowland would have burned with the rest of the village. With the League behind him, no one would be left alive.

*No*, he thought. *You wouldn't do such a thing to Liliana. Even if you desired it, you couldn't.*

*A week ago,* he countered. *A week ago, I would've done that very thing.*

With Ambrus unwilling to push away his son, Liliana's voice, distant and then closing quickly, cut the tension. Tristram watched her approach. She spoke to Rowland as one spoke to a boy.

"You're a true knight, Rowland," she said. Gracefully, she lifted the hammer from his grip. Glad for her touch, Rowland didn't protest. She looked down at Tristram. "Two knights," she said. "Rowland is the name of a knight, too, isn't it, Ambrus?"

The old man nodded impatiently.

"Rowland and Tristram," Liliana said, "about to engage in a tournament duel." She touched Rowland's begrimed hand again. "Obey your father," she told him. "This man's no match for a knight like you."

Her composure calmed him. Rowland nodded. He turned his back and started off. He lifted the helmet from his head and carried it in his hand. "Maybe I will," he said in a singsong voice. "Maybe I will, maybe I will, maybe I will."

Liliana gave the hammer to Ambrus.

"May I call you Lili?" Tristram asked. Perhaps it was the sun coupling with his fever, but her presence bewitched him completely. With the sunlight behind her red hair, she looked like an angel of mercy. She wore the wooden cross around her neck.

"You may not," Liliana said. "How do you feel, *land-sknecht?*"

Ambrus cut in. "He feels like he looks. Enough time

has been wasted. Come now." He lifted the cart by the handles and backed onto a path of crushed stone. "Chew the leather," he advised.

With Liliana at his side, Ambrus wheeled Tristram through the village.

Due to the prosperity of their trade, the community was not a huddled mass of dilapidated huts and muddy fields like so many others in the Margraviate of Brandenburg. Rather, aside from the ubiquitous smoke and hog stench, features no village escaped, the array of homes was clean and idyllic. A spired church, the first sight one took in upon approach from the road, stood at one end of the main thoroughfare. Stone rather than mud and excrement lined the footpaths. A great deal of green—canopied trees and private gardens of herbs, nightshade, and laurel— linked proud homes of wood and thatch. Mistletoe nested in the trees. Blackbirds were copious. A few dogs walked freely, well-fed pets rather than the miserable, starving jackals kept by peasants for security. Children played. A group of women stood around a boiling cauldron and open hearth, suffering the heat, preparing a communal meal.

The village was abnormally prosperous.

*How could such a place escape notice of the League?* Tristram thought. "Where are all the men?" he asked.

"There are so few men here." Ambrus admitted the weakness freely. "The war lured some away, the romantic ones. Others are in their shops, carving. A few have gone to Strausberg to market our wares. Important and vain men purchase the effigies," Ambrus went on. "For themselves and their wives and children. Barons. A few clergymen. The latter shouldn't be vain, of course." Ambrus shrugged.

"Something you have in common with Ambrus,"

Liliana said. "You both profit from death. Perchance, he's memorialized a child you've killed."

"Perchance," said Ambrus.

Bruised, Tristram asked, "Why did you save me?" He wanted to wait for a time to ask the question with more sincerity, but anger tripped him. "You performed a surgery to do so. That's a great deal of trouble for a man you scorn."

"Ambrus did those things," Liliana said. She fought emotion but her eyes betrayed her. She couldn't deny her hatred. She wanted to say more, and none of it kind.

Slowly, Tristram took his eyes off Liliana. He was staring through her, trying to fathom who she was, why she seemed alone, who had harmed her, and whom she had harmed. Unlike Ambrus, she offered no answers.

The cart stopped at a small, windowless cottage at the far edge of the village. There was something forlorn and ancient about the home, and it was less kempt than the others. The cottage had weathered many changes. A garden and forest lay beyond this final building.

"This is where you'll stay," Ambrus said. "It's important to us that you remain here."

Liliana moved to the unpainted door. A heavy branch, several inches thick, lay across two brackets, barring the entrance. It was the mark of a prison. Tristram's stomach turned. Liliana removed the branch. She opened the door outward.

Cowed by the thought of being jailed in the cottage, Tristram didn't notice that a crowd gathered behind him. When he saw, he realized an event was occurring. Even Rowland returned, wearing the breastplate. A man, equal to Ambrus in age and grayness, but smaller and frailer, separated from the crowd. Ambrus drew Tristram's attention to the man.

"This is Matthias Knock," he said. "He'll look after you."

The man, a phlegmatic tinkerer, nodded but said nothing. Arthritis left his hands gnarled.

Ambrus wheeled Tristram through the door and into the cottage. The floor was dirt with an indentation, a hole, sinking toward the center. A desire to flee did not change the situation: Tristram was unable to stand, let alone run. As Ambrus twice observed, he was weak as a foundling.

The disturbing thought that his leg didn't need severing, that the act served the same purpose as clipping bird wings, occurred to him. Tristram felt small and vulnerable under the gaze of the villagers.

He confronted the uncertainty.

"Is this revenge?" he asked Liliana.

*Whom, here, did I wrong?* he thought. It was not Ambrus. Was it Liliana? Or did Tristram, like the effigies fashioned for the dead, simply stand in representation of the things that wronged them?

Liliana, searching along the wall for a candle, said, "Far from revenge, *landsknecht.*" The words, double-edged, did not erase his despair. Liliana, unconcerned, found a tin cup of mutton fat.

Outside, the crowd moved closer to the door, held from entry by the brittle form of Matthias Knock.

"It is revenge," Tristram said.

"You're wrong," Ambrus said. "Fever is getting the best of you. You can rest easy tonight. Matthias isn't here to keep you in. He's here to keep everyone out. He'll change your bandage and clean your leg, too. It needs care. You need to sleep and gather your strength."

"For what?" Tristram asked.

Neither Ambrus nor Liliana supplied an answer.

WHEN NIGHT FELL, he lay in the cottage on a bed of straw. Fresh cloth wrapped the root of his wound. The tallow candle burned at his side, casting a halo that reached to the hole in the floor. With the heat of day still in the room a window would've been a blessing, but that was the least of his concerns. Be that as it may, he was neither gawked at nor mistreated. Enigmatic Liliana did not return. Nor did Ambrus and Rowland. Tristram was fed and given a flagon of wine. Save for a hunk of bread, which he forced down his gullet, food was not agreeable to his stomach. He kept at the wine, though, until he was drunk and morose. When he emptied one flagon, Matthias brought another. He drank the second flagon and received a third.

He had time to be alone with his thoughts, whether he desired it or not, because Matthias spoke little when he entered the cottage. The old man responded to questions with grunts, deeming nothing curious enough for words. He would walk with his head bowed and then leave quickly. The door would shut. The branch fell into place. Silence.

The cottage was an odd domicile, neither lived in nor used for storage. The structure was maintained. The roof crawled with the normal insects but allowed in no light and, judging from the condition of the walls, no rain. The floor was hardpack dirt and empty except his straw and a small cistern against one wall. The shallow hole in the center of the floor, whatever its purpose, was empty. At the bottom of the hole a plank was visible, as if dirt covered an original, lower floor.

Tristram had crawled to the hole and peered downward with the candle, and he'd seen a pictogram on the wood—a symbol he didn't recognize or understand. The symbol was a lattice of limbs and vines within a circle, a lattice like the caging that covered the effigies in Ambrus' workshop. Why someone had dug down and uncovered the pictogram made him uneasy. He had, in his travels, witnessed vigilante trials for witchcraft in poorer settlements, when old women were paraded, tortured, throttled, and burned for flaunting such icons.

The arcane symbol was not the only feature of the cottage that left him suspect. The loft above, occupying the right side of the room, held a single occupant, and it was upon this figure that Tristram stared and worried most.

Standing at the edge of the platform, near a crude ladder that descended to the floor, was the wooden statue of a cat. The alert eyes troubled him deeply. Whether a fevered thought or true, the eyes had shifted over the preceding hours, hinging steadily until they caught the candlelight and fell upon Tristram.

Unlike the animal figurines he saw previously, this cat was not frolicsome. It was not a toy. The animal was poised to strike prey: its front paws extended, its sharp claws gripping the wood, its spine arched downward, torquing strong hind legs. The tail held the impish curve of a shepherd's crook. There the animal stood, watching, waiting as hours passed.

He hoped the statue was a scarecrow fashioned to ward off rats, because rodents appeared at the base of the cottage walls frequently. These were scrawny rats the color of charcoal, occupants of every home in the countryside. The creatures never remained in sight for long, and any movement by Tristram or Matthias Knock sent them scurrying for shelter, but they were legion.

As Tristram meditated about revenge and Liliana, the cat, the rat, and the little cottage brought a rhyme to his drunken mind. He had heard his brother sing the words.

His sibling, more bookish than Tristram, learned the song from one of their father's gardeners. Percival was always collecting such baubles from common folk. In Edinburgh, Percival still collected.

The rhyme went thus:

> *There was a crooked man, and he walked a crooked mile*
> *He found a crooked sixpence upon a crooked stile.*
> *He bought a crooked cat,*
> *which caught a crooked mouse,*
> *And they all lived together in a little crooked house.*

*A fitting ode*, Tristram thought, *for a sawed-off man, newly made crooked*.

Pitifully, he laughed, and the laugh was sick and detached. His fever surged. His leg, despite fresh cloth, grew worse. Larvae squirmed inside the flesh. He could only deny the sensation for so long. The trauma of such a feeling was not the type to fade. He drank the warm wine.

He prayed Groza and the League would descend on this place. It would be glorious to thwart revenge, whatever its motivation, in its final moment. Soldiers would finish the job on Rowland and his brother, which they began in Magdeburg. The image pleased him. Who would stand and defend this village? Ambrus and Matthias? A slaughter would ensue. What a funny story it would make if Lieutenant Groza found Tristram, crooked, counting rats, and fearful of a cat in the dark.

*He would realize my condition and kill me out of mercy.*

*Why hasn't the League come to this village?* Tristram wondered again.

In his time with Groza, the League pillaged the countryside of Brandenburg thoroughly. And yet here this village stood, hidden in the open, shielded by nary a hill, wealthy, untouched, brazen, arrogant.

*What deal did these peasants make? If a deal were struck, then why fear a single* landsknecht?

*Because we hold no allegiance,* he answered, for he knew the response well. *We're dishonorable men. We fight only for money. All peasants say the same. Never did a peasant love a mercenary. Just as, Liliana would say, a peasant never loved a knight. May she be damned,* he prayed, *and by a hand other than mine.*

In the small hours of the night, after drifting in and out of a drunken, dreamless sleep, movement in the loft made Tristram sensitive to his surroundings. He lifted his eyes. Although his candle burned low, he saw that the statue's tail shifted—it dipped and straightened to a point at the end.

"Matthias," Tristram called. An urge to get free of the room seized him.

The old man did not respond. The door remained quiet.

Tristram began the rhyme in a futile attempt to calm his nerves, but the first line alone rushed through and then dissipated. *There was a crooked man*—

—The cat parted its mouth, unhinging its jaw.

"Matthias, please! Liliana! Ambrus!"

Despite his weakness, Tristram toppled from the straw, digging his elbows into the ground. A vision of absurdity, he dragged himself toward the door, using his left leg to push forward. He moved as quickly as he could, making his stomach sick with wine and pain. Only a few feet from the straw, he vomited. He crawled through the slick detritus.

The cat placed a paw on the top rung of the ladder. Tristram could not see the extent to which the statue was altered, whether its body was a coat of wood or if the exterior relaxed into fur, but the cat was animated enough to move without hindrance. It stepped downward twice before leaping to the ground. The cat, which was frozen art moments before, landed with noiseless grace. It looked at Tristram, eyes a faint yellow tinged with black, then it looked at the vomit on the floor, and then it sauntered, shoulders rolling like a panther cub, to the cavity in the center of the room. The darkened thing heaved, gargling, heaving, coughing, until it disgorged a solid lump.

The cat, matching Tristram, vomited.

Wine and bile didn't escape its stomach. The cat spewed a charcoal rat, which was neither chewed nor rent. The rodent's coat was dry. Tristram had the idea that the rat suffocated inside the wooden statue. The image of encasement was devastating.

Tristram called for Matthias again. When he reached the door, he hammered his fist against oak. He grabbed the handle and shoved. The door did not give. He battered the planks until his hands were bruised. He listened but heard nothing on the other side.

He didn't have to wonder long about how the rat became encased within the statue. The cat, ignoring Tristram's presence, walked to the farthest wall. One of the rats, mesmerized, stood idle. A small pool of urine spread beneath it, darkening the ground. The cat unhinged its jaw like a snake, opening its mouth impossibly wide, and ate the rodent. The cat's throat bulged and then regained its original shape.

Without struggle, the cat swallowed.

"Matthias," Tristram called through the door, weakly.

Gingerly as it had come, the cat stalked to the ladder and climbed to the loft. Once it had assumed its original pose, shepherd's crook tail included, the cat ceased movement and grew rigid. Its eyes, their luminescence the last remnant of life to depart, found the straw empty and then drifted to the door where Tristram lay. There the eyes stopped and remained.

———————

LILIANA REMOVED the bar and opened the cottage door, allowing in morning light. She looked down at the soiled form of Tristram, pale as death, and she hummed a familiar melody. It was another rhyme from his childhood, another song Percival collected, about a lascivious, murderous knight. She sang:

> *An arrogant knight came from the highlands*
> *And he came a'wooing of me*
> *He told me he'd take me to the highlands*
> *And there he would marry me*
> *"Lie there, lie there, you false-hearted man,*
> *Lie there instead of me,*
> *For if six pretty maidens thou hast slain*
> *The seventh has slain thee."*

She knelt, red hair untwined and resplendent and falling to her shoulders. Rather than a greeting, she asked, "Did you see it?" Her face was eager.

Tristram struggled to a sitting position. His leg had bled profusely through the cloth, having dragged hard against the dirt. The bandage was soiled and full of worms. Vomit had hardened in his beard and crusted his lips. His eyes were ringed red.

Impatiently, she asked, "Did you see it?"

He nodded. "How do you know that song?" he asked, his mind dreadfully heavy. "My brother sang it. My brother," he said, "always sang little songs like that. Did you know him?"

It was a mad question, and the fact that he asked it frightened him. Internally and externally, he was disconnected. He watched himself slip away. He tried to draw the question back inside, and that, too, was mad.

"You talk in your sleep," Liliana said. "Sometimes you sing. You saw it, didn't you? Did it perform?"

"The crooked cat?"

Liliana smiled, deeply pleased. That was enough.

"Rowland," she called.

*Yes,* he thought. *It performed quite the trick. The poor rat. The crooked rat. The crooked man. The crooked cat. The crooked house.*

The statue came to life and consumed.

Heavy footsteps approached on gravel. Armor scraped.

Tristram sighed. He had no strength to do anything else.

"Fetch your father and Matthias," Liliana said. "He's the right one." She touched Tristram's face and said, "Save your strength, *landsknecht.* Tonight you'll see another trick."

"To whom do you pray?" Tristram asked. "I found the symbol on the floor, Lili. You're a sorceress, are you not?"

Liliana proffered the cross she wore.

"Far from it," she said.

"Then why do this?"

Liliana put her mouth to his ear. Her breath was hot.

"To save us," she whispered. Then, as Ambrus, Rowland, and Matthias came near, she sang softly,

> *"Lie there, lie there, you false-hearted man,*
> *Lie there instead of me."*

As they had done before, but with less concern for his pain, Ambrus and Rowland lifted Tristram from the ground and placed him in the vegetable cart. It was a pitiful ritual. Rowland wore the helmet again, and now battered gauntlets covered his forearms, and greaves his shins. He carried a mallet in place of a sword. The dinted breastplate shone in the sun, making him a gross carica-ture. He lifted the handles of the cart and steered it toward the other homes of the village.

Liliana, elated, without remorse, led the procession.

"He'll do," she said, as people emerged. She spoke with authority. "He was accepted. He'll do."

There were many voices, but one refrain from the throng reached him, a faceless voice, that of a woman: "Praise her and protect us, Lord. Praise this dearest of goddesses. She, too, is your child."

*No. You're damning yourselves,* he thought. *All of you.*

Infectious merriment spread through the amassing crowd, but all this passed in a blur for Tristram. He tried to roll free from the cart, but Rowland struck him hard behind the ear, a hammering blow he couldn't withstand in his condition, and he ceased the fight. He was dead weight, barely able to lift a hand. He began to slip under, and he wondered again about whom he had wronged.

"Bring it forward, Ambrus," Liliana said.

Ambrus moved, carrying the large effigy of a man beneath his arm. The figure wore a limb and vine cage over its head. The dangling arms, jointed at the shoulder, elbow, and wrist, moved freely. When he reached Liliana, Ambrus unclasped the mask and handed it to her. Fungus soiled the back of the effigy's head, like a stone in the forest. Ambrus carried the wooden man to the cottage at the end of the lane. He dipped inside, untroubled.

Liliana, carrying the mask, leaned toward Tristram.

"Tonight," she said, "you're the rat, brave knight. You're the rat. And the wooden man is the cat."

"Groza's army will come. You can't do this to all of them."

"No," Liliana admitted, "we can't do this to all of them. This will keep him away, though. For a decade it's kept armies away."

"Sorceress," he said.

"Far from it, *landsknecht*." She placed the pungent mask on his face to quiet him.

# 4

# A PANTHEON OF THIEVES

**G**erard and North watched from the shoreline, holding flashlights, casting yellow beams over coal-dark water. The lights resembled shuddering eyes.

Price stepped through a swirl of mud where the water reached his chest, and he gripped the floating body. It was midnight in hot August, and Price held a bloated corpse by its ragged ankles. He walked backwards over slick beds of twigs and leaves, pulling the weight, struggling to keep his balance.

"Don't tell me it's all rot," North said.

His light found the swollen face. The corpse had slits in place of eyes, two parallel indentations rather than a nose, and a purple mouth that had crumbled. Chunks of black and gray flesh were eaten away.

Price recoiled, and his eyes darted to the water. Even if the stench didn't raise his vomit, the pulpy face would. He choked back the urge, tightening his grip, twisting loose flesh under his palms.

Price backed until the water was at his ankles. When he

was clear of the lake, he dropped the legs into the mud. Gerard and North pushed him aside and knelt by the dead man. They exchanged excited glances over the body.

"Is there enough?" Price asked. His breath was heavy.

North peered over his shoulder. The moon, a crescent, shone in the lenses of his glasses.

"I can't say," he started.

"There is," Gerard said. "I feel it."

Price felt something, too, but the energy was difficult to cage and understand. He was distant. He looked over the lake. The tree line reflected from one side of the water to the other, ripples of moon breaking the image. He looked at his hands. Specks of gray skin glistened on his palms. With disgust renewed, Price washed his hands in the water.

"It's strong," Gerard said. He breathed deeply.

North listened, but Price kept his back to the scene, pretending distraction.

*We're little gods*, he thought, *stealing secrets from dead men.*

He picked a ghost-white patch of skin from his shirt, dropped the flap into the lake, and then he watched the flesh teeter on a wave.

*But such secrets*, he thought, submerging his hands.

---

"WE CAN DO IT HERE," Gerard said. "There's no need to wait."

Fire shadows pinched his features, giving him a rat face behind his blond beard. He wiped a veined forearm across his nose, smearing sweat. The fire, unnecessary in the muggy air, was intended for Price. Gerard and North sat ten feet from the blaze, at the edge of the flickering halo.

The lake was sublime, waiting beneath a stand of

walnut trees. The corpse, the consistency of wet concrete, lay on a tarp.

"We should have the protection of the van," North said. "Put up a wall or two for your sake."

"For your sake." Gerard stared past the fire.

"Get it over with," Price cut in. "I'd rather not drag him to the goddamn van."

Gerard nodded.

North wasn't satisfied. He grimaced.

"What if he gets in your head? What if he stares back into you? We don't know what'll happen next."

"No," Gerard agreed, "but a Chrysler won't stop him. If the connection's made, I can't be anymore naked and vulnerable."

"You know what I mean," North said.

A thin, nervous man in his sixties, North once made a living teaching parapsychology courses.

"What was his real name?" Price asked. He watched the bloated man as he spoke. Frogs croaked across the lake.

North turned. "We call him Enoch, but his real name is Sollima. He was born in Chicago in '59. He was a student of mine in the 80s. He flunked out, and I went after him when he left. There was nothing quite like his mind until Gerard came along."

"Can you read what I'm thinking?" Price asked.

He stuck his hands to the fire, watching Gerard over the licking flame. He'd tested the telepath on a few occasions. He found the man stiff, humorless, and lacking personality beyond the shifting moods his eyes betrayed.

Gerard nodded. His face was worn. He had no need to elaborate.

"I want to begin," he said finally. "We're not going back."

"Very well," North said. He stood, wiping sand from

his pants. "We'll begin."

Crickets thrummed. A thick limb split in the fire, sending burning dust skyward.

———

It was January 1982, cold even by Wisconsin standards. A clock that read 2:13 all the time hung above the doorway. Enoch entered the classroom with two sheets of crumpled paper in his fist. He didn't speak. He never spoke anymore.

North stood in a labyrinth of chemistry workstations, his hands against an overturned stool. Enoch's thoughts traveled. The point was a hammer stroke to North.

"Don't," North said feebly. Then, slowly, "You're needed here."

*I want* one *thing in this world.*

"I want that."

*Not for the reason you want it.*

"Enoch, please. Consider it another week. *One week.*"

Enoch turned in the doorway. He had become so righteous over the course of a year.

North ran, nearly grabbing the young man by the shoulder. He stopped out of fear, a threat of harm staying his hand.

"I'll pay you for your notes. Any price you require."

Enoch continued into the whitewashed corridor, passing a row of benches and frosted windows. North followed.

"Anything."

Enoch closed his mind and became a walking shape.

North would follow him for the rest of his life, and he knew that fact then, standing alone in the hallway. He had to know. He wondered if Enoch listened to his begging.

PRICE, clothes heavy, cold, and damp, listened, but he found nothing except North's heavy breathing to break the silence. Gerard was a statue between the trees, his hand over Enoch's forehead. An hour had passed with the two telepaths, one dead, one alive, searching for the slivers of energy to forge a connection.

Price wasn't schooled on North's theory, because the professor wouldn't spill details. But the idea, the thing over which North obsessed, was that Gerard would pilfer the remains of Enoch's mind. Whether the memories and ideas were navigable, only Gerard could say. If so, then someone with Gerard's talent could unpack the details.

North, a brown fedora pulled low to his glasses, kept one hand against the back of his neck. Price had met the scholar in an unlikely place: on the littered midway of a country carnival. Price, no telepath, had two talents: he could steal a revolver from a policeman's hip, and he could pick up on energy, lock it in his brain, and follow it anywhere. The former bought him lunch, the latter put a decent pillow under his head.

Price had tracked Enoch for thirteen months, only to find a cryptic suicide note at the end of the line. The body wasn't in the motel room with the handwritten scribble. Until now, the body had not been found. Price put his nose to the ground. North brought Gerard, and together the three had entered the forest.

Enoch was satisfied in taking his secret to the grave. North was slow in revealing what the secret entailed, but he finally broke the seal, allowing Price the knowledge while the two passed a bottle of cheap scotch around another campfire in another summer. Enoch knew a method for gifting telepathic ability to otherwise untalented individuals. He could make a blind man see, in a sense. North admitted the idea made his mouth water. He studied the power because he desired it. Enoch had expressed a piece of the theory to North outside a Wisconsin coffee shop, under a canopied table with bicyclists stirring leaves and cars whirring at stop signs. But only a piece. Enoch became obsessed with the theory. North became obsessed with the sliver he possessed.

Now, with heavy payment owed to Gerard, he looked to steal the fully developed ideas.

Gerard stirred in the shadows, finally lifting his gaze, rising to his knees. His eyes were like melting glass. Price moved from the fire. North slid his palm from his neck and stilled his breath. As suspense mounted, Gerard parted his lips, swallowed, and then fainted cold, planting his face into the mush of death with a slap.

---

"WHAT'D YOU FIND?" North asked. He smacked Gerard's cheek.

Price cupped water from the lake, and then, with droplets seeping between his knuckles, he splashed Gerard's face. Specks of Enoch's skin stood out on his lips, nose, and chin. His shoulder flinched at the touch of water, and then his head swayed to one side. Gerard blinked to life. Rising on his elbow, he vomited.

"Christ," Price said.

On his knees, North leaned closer.

Gerard wiped his mouth. "Throw Enoch in the water," he said weakly. "Get the fuck rid of him."

"What'd you read?" North asked. He barely contained himself. His hands trembled.

Gerard kicked at the tarp under his feet, then he struggled to stand. He looked around, nearly buckling at the knees, turning a circle before looking down at North.

"He's too close, goddamnit. Get him away!"

North nodded at Price.

"Do what?" Price asked.

"Get the corpse away. Take it into the water." North turned to Gerard. "Did you find what I need?"

"I'm okay," Gerard said shakily. He put his hands against his knees, then he wiped his palms clean against denim.

Price dragged the tarp to the tree line, dropping it before Enoch's body. He knelt, found leverage against the shoulder, and then he flipped the corpse onto the tarp. Energy pulsed from the body, seeping like a barrier had fissured. In his time following Enoch, Price had never felt the man's energy so strongly or negatively. Dread stalked every web of the aura. Price considered dropping the entire act and running into the forest—running anywhere. The thought was tempting, but he dragged Enoch toward his watery grave. The heavy tarp scraped dirt. Price stopped to listen when Gerard spoke again.

The voice was unusually soft and thoughtful. "I saw...." He stopped. "It was awful, North."

North fidgeted.

Gerard cried. Vomit speckled his beard. If not for the heavy air, and the heavy dark, the man would've been ridiculous, but now he was in touch with something no one else understood.

"Tell me," North begged.

"It was decay, but physical turned mental, like thoughts with teeth. It wasn't dark like you'd think. A burst of brilliant points of color. Full, deep colors, but all dots, and millions of them. I locked onto him. It wasn't even a search. His energy just came forward. I was paralyzed in it."

"What else? What about his memories?"

Gerard shook his head. "I don't know."

North stood and paced. "What do you mean, you don't know?"

"I saw a thousand snippets. Countless thoughts, but the ideas had decayed. Nothing was full. It may come back to me, but it's a blur. I see the light mostly. I feel him, but the thoughts are incomplete. Price?"

Price, holding Enoch's feet through the tarp, stood erect in the shoreline mud.

"Sink him," Gerard said. "Please."

"What's the corpse have to do with it?" North asked.

"The connection isn't dropping." Gerard grimaced. "It should be. He was telepathic, so it's linked and holding. The decay keeps coming on."

"Sink him," North ordered.

Price steeled himself, and then he entered the water. The cold wrapped his bones. Shock was a welcome diversion from the assault of energy pouring from the corpse. He understood what Gerard said. The thing Gerard felt in his mind, Price felt over his skin, down to his nerves. The decay was palpable.

With Enoch afloat, Price placed one arm over the waist, allowed the tarp to float free, then swam toward the deep, distant center. The fire burned over his shoulder, and he turned back periodically to glance at the silhouette figures, one pacing, one sitting with face buried, by the flame. He paddled and kicked, treading water. The night was quiet. No frogs, no crickets now. The moon cast light on the lake.

"Price!"

The voice came distantly. Price turned, not realizing

he'd drifted so close to the middle. North was a speck on the shore, a dark slant. He shouted again, but the words didn't carry.

The corpse loosened its form, wobbling on the waves. Price kept his arm tight over the waist, ignoring North, searching for the coil of rope in his satchel.

*It's the way the water rocks*, Price thought uneasily, *that makes Enoch move.*

The corpse's arm moved away from the body, stretching out, reaching.

North continued to shout.

"What?!!" Price countered.

North stopped to listen. His waving arms dwindled.

"Fucking Christ," Price said. He spat water.

Enoch's finger curled, grazing Price's elbow. He jumped from the water, slackening his hold. Enoch's head creaked at the neck, and the face lifted. The swollen visage, featureless save for gashes, stared forward.

Jolted with terror, Price released his grip and shoved away the corpse. Enoch bobbed with the water, his head raised, his finger extended, while Price swam away. He swam hard toward the shore, swallowing scummy water as it washed into his mouth. He choked, struggling to breathe. His arms and legs kept moving until he reached the stamped mud. A wave washed in behind him, pushing up the shore toward the fire.

North looked down, his face pallid.

Price, struggling for air, coughing, looked over the water. The dark corpse, with a strip of moonlight across its rotten torso, floated with an uncoiled rope like a snake at its side.

"Where's Gerard?" Price asked, turning back. He tried to push Enoch's restless body from his mind.

"He ran," North said. He looked defeated and

frightened.

"What did he say?"

"Nothing, but he screamed like murder."

———

THE VAN, parked on the shoulder of Route Seven, hadn't moved. The door was locked, the windows intact, but Price sensed Gerard had been by and would return. A gust of wind pushed through the curve in the road behind, shaking trees. A few leaves rained down. Overripe walnuts slapped the asphalt.

The breeze was chilling against Price's soaked clothes. After sloshing to the front of the van, he met North's gaze.

"Are you picking up on him?" North asked. He adjusted the lenses on the bridge of his nose.

Price pulled keys from his pocket. He unlocked the van's side door and slid it open. Then he sat on the carpeted floor, hanging his feet over the running board and onto the roadside gravel. He hadn't smoked in four years, but he wanted to light up.

"Did it ever occur to you, North, that you're blinding as fog to people like me?"

North didn't answer.

A scream echoed in the distance.

"Or to guys like Enoch. Or Gerard. You're damn demanding."

"I'm a child to you. What else would you expect?" North asked smugly.

Price stared at the ground. "He's coming back. I sense that much."

On cue, Gerard appeared in the bend of the road. He stumbled, holding his head and letting forth an awful shriek, casting a silhouette against headlights that approached from behind. Gerard stopped, dropped his hands, and stared as a pickup sped by. Taillights, and then the hum of the engine, faded in the distance.

Price started up the road. North took the lead when the men stood before the telepath.

Gerard screamed again, doubling at the waist.

"Stop it," he growled. "Stop it!"

He screeched like his lungs were broken glass.

North touched his shoulder. "What the hell's wrong with you?"

Gerard straightened, swallowed hard. "It hurts," he said. "And it's… it's…." The words ended in a babble of tears.

A memory wobbled Price. Words not so cryptic now. Enoch's final rambling letter to the world contained a line that had troubled Price, although he couldn't, at the time, break its code. It was a warning amidst goodbye.

*The creator retakes the flame—but the thief? May he be burned.*

*Enoch's ability to gift telepathy is the flame. Gerard is the thief. And the creator? Enoch.*

"Enoch isn't dead," Price blurted.

North withdrew his hand and turned his back on Gerard. "What?"

"This isn't an accident. It's a punishment."

"No. No, it's not that at all," North said. "Gerard, tell me what you see. Try."

Gerard whimpered.

"Gerard! Tell me what you see!"

His voice trickled forth.

"Lights and a razor scraping the inside of my skull." Raising his head, he was momentarily lucid. "It's his death. He's giving his death to me."

Gerard bolted, splitting Price and North and heading for the van. He disappeared through the door.

North gave chase, but Price didn't bother. He watched and waited. Before North reached the back wheels, a flash of orange, and an explosive report, rocked the Chrysler's frame, lighting the windows. Then another shot. Then silence.

North stopped running.

*He found the gun*, Price thought.

---

EARLY MORNING COVERED THE FOREST. The lake was peaceful. The air was humid, thick with hungry insects.

"It's a damn waste is all," North said.

Price kicked dirt over the ashes, kicked angrily until every trace of the fire was gone. He'd been ill since seeing Gerard in the blood-splattered van. Immense guilt left him uncommunicative.

"What did you mean when you said he didn't die?" North asked.

"In his letter," Price said softly, trying to control his mood. "He talked about this."

"So, he protected himself. That doesn't mean he's alive."

Price shrugged. "Maybe not. But where's the body?" he asked, pointing over the lake.

"At the bottom, thank God."

"I don't think it was one way. When Gerard tapped in, Enoch stole something back. Both were thieves. Enoch still had life in his bones."

"He had no reason."

"He had you. Your torment."

North stared. "What do you want me to say? That Gerard's my fault? Okay, it's my fault. Enoch? He's my fault, too."

"Yet you're still standing."

"Here." North walked to the shoreline and placed his hands on either side of his mouth. He shouted over the water. "Enoch! I'm sorry." Frowning, he turned back. "That better?" North looked so weak when he was falling under, and so proud at the same time.

The water moved. A breeze crossed the serene face, lifting a wave toward the shore. All around, leaves showed their white underbellies. The wave touched the shore. Price felt familiar energy in the air. He stepped back. North watched the water with his usual cryptic fascination.

Enoch washed ashore.

He was no more alive than when Price fished him from the lake. Maybe he was truly dead, but his body had moved dramatically, even intelligently. With one arm at his side, Enoch had stretched the other arm forward, bending his hand into a claw. The claw fell into a footprint in the mud. One leg, too, was bent at the knee with the foot curling for a grip. Enoch had sunk to the bottom, struggled in the muck, and then pulled himself forward—toward what?

"Gerard knew," Price said.

He was cold to his marrow. A fly dropped from the air and landed on the corpse, traveling its shoulder.

North never twitched, never removed his eyes from the body. His lips parted as his jaw fell open. A look of awe for some, but a look of deep terror for Professor North.

Enoch's bloated face had calmed, the swelling had receded, and two black sclerae with the shine of polished onyx stared through folds of graying skin. The eyes were dead, yet they held a distinct spark.

*The mask of a thief*, thought Price, *both conceals and threatens*.

# 5

# UNDEAD HELLCATS

The night Repo was hit we tried to hide it. Going for the cops was a fool thing to do, especially with the way they were hounding me, so we put Repo in a car and drove out of the city. The hospital was no good, not with a net around it, so we drove. As the night faded, my liquor haze passed. After an hour, nobody in the car was high.

We watched Repo dying, which was a bad thing to see. The kid went from clutching his stomach and screaming to trying to accept the pain to blacking out. Between spells, he moaned and asked for his mom. He kept his hands at his stomach like that was the thing holding in his guts. Maybe it was.

I stared through Repo, and deep inside I was scared.

Those new kids, the Schizos, always had guns. I think each of them carried two fully loaded pistols. A month ago, we gave the first of them a good swift kick in the ass. He was in the wrong neighborhood that day, talking to the wrong girl. He was the only one I've ever seen without a gun. Maybe he was there to get things moving. He said things. We kicked his skull until the skin opened under his black hair. He said things about a new gang in town. Repo stomped his wrist.

*Schizos*, he said.

*Schizos?*

He was barely breathing. I was amazed he could talk.

*We're takin' over.*

*Schizos?*

Imagine a boy with blood on his face, saying that to you from the ground. It was damn funny. We all had a good laugh about it. He was the first of them but not the last, and the ones that followed had guns. They also had eyes for our girls, like that was the one way they knew they could get us fighting. We went in to fight them in the old style, but they didn't want any of that. They weren't in it to throw punches. They just pulled guns and let loose. They killed two juniors the first time. We took them up again tonight, and Repo got one in the stomach. Jackie got a trench cut in his thigh. As my mother would say, Providence saved me. I wasn't even grazed. I was lucky.

We drove around until Repo quit breathing. Somewhere out in the country, somewhere near the old prison and the steel mill hulks, we shoved his body in a culvert. The water ran under his back, and when it came out by his head there was blood in it.

"I'll kill them," I said, but not even the boys believed me.

———

THAT WAS SATURDAY NIGHT. Now it's Tuesday morning, and I see Repo in the street below my window, walking around with no light in his eyes.

*Repo. Dead in the culvert.*

the machinery, Pilot. Might as well be dinosaur bones in a museum."

Penn was, he claimed, an enthusiast and collector of radio technology. What he did in life was anybody's guess. So far, his expertise didn't result in much help. The idea that a radio wave was the only way of getting a signal off the planet brought Harris more despair. Only the military worked with radio, and he had particularly bad feelings about the military, despite his father's nostalgia.

To be rescued by the military was as good as enlistment. Nothing was free.

"What'd you see out there?" Mr. Dylan, Penn's companion, asked.

"The valley's nothing but frozen fog," Harris said. "I couldn't see the stars. And the transport—" He broke off, experiencing the crush of the news again.

"I see what you're thinking, Pilot," said Brisbane.

Penn and Mr. Dylan sneered, and Mr. Dylan, the bumpkin with no first name, harrumphed.

"The old fart couldn't get a signal beyond the wall, let alone through the fog, even if his equipment were pristine. I tend to agree with you." Brisbane's features were emotionless, but somehow his eyes smiled.

*Creep,* Harris thought.

The freak's veins pulsed. "Given time and energy, I could reach someone. Transports pass through this route often, do they not?"

Harris shrugged. "Every 20 hours." The probe of Brisbane's thoughts, the feeling of invasion, left him uncomfortable. Most freaks had the tact to be silent about their perusal, but Brisbane made his presence known.

Penn defended his talent with radio, but no one, including his companion, acknowledged him. He'd had his chance.

"What do you need?" Harris asked.

He was close enough to the fire that it was painful. He wrung his hands in the blistering heat. The wall trembled with mounting gales. Beyond the glow of firelight, the temperature dropped. Thoughts of his father and the Ice Garden crept into Harris, and a feeling of terror underlay them. The idea of blood freezing in the vein. The shatter of a pulse.

Brisbane considered. "I'll need Penn and Dylan's share of food." Again, his eyes did the smiling.

The last wall of Penn's bigotry crumbled.

"Where we come from," he started, "there's only one thing to do with abominations like you."

"Pray tell," Brisbane said. As he spoke, he projected a thought into Harris: *Your share, too. I'll need it all, in fact. To the last of it.* The projection was a demonstration of talent, the first time he'd gone so far.

Mr. Dylan provided the details, but Brisbane had heard the threat before. He was more amused than intimidated—such was the life of a freak.

*We'll take the gamble,* Harris thought. *What else is there to do?*

Brisbane smiled.

---

If measured in seasons, Alta Montane had experienced twenty-two thaws since the last stirring, being twenty-two rotations around a distant sun. Up to then, men, in their small way, had conquered the icescape, marring the valleys with way stations and fortresses. Man's presence here had, from the start, been of a military nature. The caged satellites in orbit said as much, as did the mountaintop machinery aimed toward thin sheets of ozone. There was nothing to gain but territory in the settlement of Alta Montane.

Twenty-two thaws since the last stirring, and several hundred thaws since the one prior, but the Great Old One that moved under the ice and in the mountains was not calendar conscious. There was no rhythm to His actions. He moved when He moved. Sometimes He acted, and sometimes He reacted. Such was His cycle.

WHEN BRISBANE SLEPT—HIS small frame coiled under a stack of blankets and a tarp—the fire ebbed and nearly died. The conflagration was one of many dreams in the freak's mind, so the fire behaved according to the attention he paid it. Sometimes a stray image from Brisbane's dreams formed in the single flame. Most often these were faces too shadowy to identify. Presently, the flame produced the warmth of a candle, and its cone of light was measured in inches. It had been thus for hours, while Brisbane, stuffed gluttonously, built up precious energy and strength. He intended to project a distress call into the flight zone that passed beyond Alta Montane's orbit. To do so, he required optimal strength.

In full gear, but without additional garments for warmth, Harris began to freeze. The cold was unrelenting, and the wall proved frailer by the minute. He wondered how long his heart would hold out. He wondered how long it would take for his blood to freeze. Numbness spread from his digits into his arms and legs— the lack of sensation crept toward his core. Huddling with Penn and Mr. Dylan, he conserved warmth through silence.

Mr. Dylan broke the monotony of wind and dark. His

whisper was a cloud of frost, only the edge of which caught the faint light.

"Pilot, it could be that dying is a better option than allowing our freak to perform."

Harris gave no response. His eyes were opaque.

What could be said? The transport's gadgetry was reduced to scrap metal, the fortress's machinery decayed to dinosaur bones. Brisbane was their only chance of survival. Either the freak fished a passerby with whatever faculties lay beneath his ugly, tattooed skull or he did not. There was nothing else to do except freeze, but Dylan was deaf to sensible thinking. Paranoia drove him.

"Tell me this, Pilot," Mr. Dylan said. It was a defense he'd been preparing. "Have you heard the stories about Alta Montane?"

Here was truth rather than bigotry.

Harris nodded curtly. *Like the Ice Garden*, he thought. The stories were similar. The thing his father had spoken about once but never again. *The eye that opened on the battlefield, the eye that was mistaken for a moon.*

*The Frost Giant*, his father said. *They called it a Frost Giant.*

Penn joined. "That doesn't disturb you, Pilot?"

Mr. Dylan pulled the men closer, lowering his voice still more.

"There's a damn good reason this place is abandoned, and it isn't the cold. Some of the soldiers were left living, you know. Some were evacuated. Do you know what they say, Pilot?"

"I know," Harris admitted. One couldn't travel the Alta system and not know. The soldiers talked openly of what they saw. A few soldiers lived on Alta Sub-Four.

"I wasn't entirely truthful," Penn said. "The equipment's not only old. The radio was intentionally destroyed.

They smashed it up before they left. All that time ago, Pilot, that was the last thing they did here."

"They say sending out radio signals was like a rat poking its head from its nest," Mr. Dylan said. "Those soldiers were the rats. You think that freak sending out whatever the hell he has is different? It may be that freezing to death is better, Pilot. It may be. You know what they say about the soldiers that lived. I've seen them."

"We'd at least have the satisfaction to watch one of his kind shrivel and wither away." Penn nodded at Brisbane. "Seeing that, I'd die somewhat close to happy."

"Do you know what happened to the soldiers that lived, Pilot?" Mr. Dylan persisted.

Harris was silent. He wondered why his father had spoken of it only once. Why he spoke of it at all.

"Do you?"

---

MEMORIES OF ALTA SUB-FOUR:

*He was weak then, a frail child. Despite his guardian's assurance that Alta Montane was a dot in the enormous sky, he had profound doubt. His guardian, an old woman who replaced his mother on his Day of Reaping, blamed his doubt on a mix of arrogance and ignorance, the bane of the gifted. Her people, she reminded him, and she led many, would rely on him when the time came.*

*She had nursed his talent, and she would continue to do so, but he must believe. That was foundational. He must learn to follow.*

*Her hand, with dark nubs where fingers had been, brushed the sky and stopped at the pinpoint called Alta Montane. She used his mother's name, Brisbane, when she addressed him, and he felt a pang at its careful pronunciation. He had to conquer his feelings. He was more than a son—and his mother and father were acquiescent in this process. The guardian's other hand, less mutilated, caressed the*

77

*knobbed skin of his baldpate. His mother came here for a reason. She is compliant, he reminded himself.*

Again, *the guardian said,* recite.

The Great Old One, *the child droned.* Bravgh-Chry, Giant of the Frost.

Again.

Bravgh-Chry.

Do you see him? Look inward. Not out there. Look inside. Do you see the others? Your companions that day?

*He looked inward. Couched in the tangle of images, he saw something. Under a layer of darkness, the ice moved. There was a growing fissure, a wall, stillness in the air, and darkness. What he mistook for a mountain in the distance moved nearer.*

*Around the guardian, and around the boy, a shadowy group murmured.*

Again, *she said,* recite.

*Through recitation and vision, the boy came to believe, trust, and follow.*

---

WHEN BRISBANE AWOKE and climbed from beneath his pile of blankets, the fire grew tall and bright. Like starved animals faced with food, Harris, Penn, and Mr. Dylan, numb and delirious, embraced the heat. Their circle tightened around the flame. It was the relief of water in the desert.

Outside, night begot night, but the wind calmed. Frost and snow settled in the darkness.

Brisbane was no more generous than he'd been upon his retirement hours prior. He wrapped the blankets around his shoulders and sat on the ground with his legs crossed. Only the tarp lay unused.

Penn, with little hesitation, fetched it. Wearing it as a

cape, he returned to the fire. Soon, Mr. Dylan shared the tarp. Lost in reflection, Brisbane ignored them.

*He's much like a vampire*, Mr. Dylan had said. *Growing strong at our expense.*

Looking down at the freak, Harris agreed. By the hour, his faith in the creature's ability to save them decreased. He wondered if trusting Brisbane was a mistake. What if the freak were only trying to outlast the others, to hold out longer? There were tales on Alta Sub-Four about Brisbane's kind—tales of sacrifice and cannibalism—the kind of ludicrous story that vexed Mr. Dylan and Penn. Harris contained his anger and impatience, but he formed the question foremost in his thoughts, and he put it to the freak.

"When?" Harris asked.

Brisbane's veins moved like worms over his skull. His eyes remained on the fire.

"What is the Ice Garden?" he asked. "You keep thinking about it."

"Take a peek at what I'm thinking," Penn mumbled.

*That's not proof that you can do what you're saying you can do,* Harris thought. *I'm not impressed. If you don't act, we'll all be dead soon. The three of us, at least.*

*Isn't it proof?* Brisbane countered. *What'd your father see? You don't have to say it aloud.*

With concentration, Harris blanked his thoughts, but it was energy ill spent.

*Did your father ever visit Alta Sub-Four?*

*He didn't.*

*But he did. When I was a child, he was there. He spoke to me. He told me the same story he told you.*

"I'm ready to begin," Brisbane said. "Pilot, accompany me to the watchman's station." He looked at Penn and Mr. Dylan. "Remain here."

Penn edged closer to his companion. Beneath the tarp, their hands were clasped.

Although it pained Harris to leave the fire, he assented. He lowered the hard mask against his face. Without word, he led Brisbane to the foot of the grated stairs, and then he climbed to the top of the wall. His footfalls echoed.

Wrapped in blankets, the freak followed.

It was jarring to find no light coating the icescape with the turn of morning. The persistent darkness of the planet was troubling, with or without the cold.

When his eyes adjusted, Harris scanned the field at the base of the wall, then he searched in the distance for mountains. Cutting wind had blown away the shroud of fog. The night was clear and crystallized. Above, he saw the stars in detail. The stars looked wrong, however, out of place, rearranged. Harris reasoned that it was better to not look at the sky. He trembled as numbness returned to his fingers.

"The stirring began with a crack in the ice," Brisbane said. "That's how the soldiers told it, isn't that right?"

A blanket covered his skull like a monk's cowl. His withered, pale skin, his thin nose, his slight mouth were barely visible. He spoke from within the folds.

"The soldiers in this very structure and the soldiers at the Ice Garden. You've compared the stories, haven't you? Somewhere deep down, perhaps in the twilight before sleep, and you didn't realize it. It was an unforgettable experience for them. A religious experience. That's why your father had to tell you. Even if only once, he had to tell you."

"How'd you know him?" Harris asked.

"Let me show you something."

Harris followed the path of Brisbane's outstretched hand. The freak pointed at a crack in the ice at the base of the wall. As Harris stared, the crack grew five feet, then five more, like a wire yanked from dirt. The fracture snaked beneath the wall.

Clatter issued from below. If Penn and Mr. Dylan scrambled from the growing maw, they avoided the stairs. Harris had a sick feeling about his companions. He had a vision, his own or one planted by Brisbane, of Penn and Mr. Dylan swallowed, simply gone. He listened for them but heard nothing.

"Look away and it will stop. Look again and it will move."

Harris did as he was told and found what the freak said was true. The crack grew when he looked at it. When he looked away, it stopped.

"It's only real if there's an audience. Even the Old Ones have limitations."

"Do your work," Harris said, his voice muffled. "There's no need to waste your energy on tricks." Regardless, Harris chanced a look at the crack below once more. As he did, it grew. He looked away and it stopped. He fought the fear that grew in his mind. He ignored reality.

"Tell me of the eye that opened on your father and his men," Brisbane continued. "The eye that could've been a moon."

Harris considered lifting Brisbane's slight frame and throwing the creature to the ice. It would be suicide, but he couldn't deny the appeal. He nearly made the effort, but what followed stunned him into inaction.

With surprising strength, Brisbane pulled Harris close.

"I work best in my sleep," he said. "I called him. I called him forth. Look up. It's only real when there's an audience. Look up!"

An eye, higher than the distant mountains, opened.

Alta Montane trembled and cracked. There was movement in the ice and above it. A consuming force filled the darkness. Harris realized he hadn't been looking at stars, and the realization snapped a cord in his mind.

---

*GLIMPSES OF ALTA SUB-FOUR:*

Alta Sub-Four possessed beautiful forests. In the isolated regions, where forests were protected from destruction for a millennium, the only way to navigate the trails was by foot or, for the skilled, by spurring a pack animal. Much of the beauty was engineered, with foresters transplanting exotic plants from all over the Alta system. Even though one saw the hazy skyline of Alta Sub-Four's cityscapes from the peaks of hills, the urban world disappeared and was forgotten in the lush, green valleys.

Here, travelers sought peace and solitude.

Occasionally, the initiated sought more. The cult of Bravgh-Chry sent those with desires of initiation here on a pilgrim's circuit.

Presently, two travelers on foot, two women, moved down a rocky slope toward a man standing in the shadow of a tree. He was aware of their presence and didn't flee, which boded well. As their hearts trembled, the women advanced across a trail covered by sunlight. Dirt broke beneath their steps.

The man (he was handsome once, but now his face was skull-like, his skin thin enough to tear) looked around with trepidation.

*He is the wanderer,* the travelers agreed. *Harris, the Pilot, one of the broken-minded.*

*You are holy to us,* they said.

The women showered the man with platitudes. There

was, they knew, an image of Bravgh-Chry in his mind, burned there. He'd seen the beatific.

Unmoved, the man turned his eyes to the ground.

*You were with him. You were with Brisbane, the Prophet.*

*Tell us: what happened to Brisbane? What happened to your companions?*

*Consumed,* the Pilot said.

Men in the city—men who'd revealed the secrets of initiation and foreshadowed the pilgrims' circuit—were correct. Of the countless many who put the question to Harris, *consumed* was the only answer returned. Although there were more questions, Harris, the Pilot, turned from the trail and navigated a tangle of roots into the deeper forest. He mumbled unintelligible things.

*His father, too, beheld, although with less directness. His father was not broken. There's great strength in his line. To see fully and only break? To see fully and not be consumed?*

One could only aspire to achieve what Harris achieved. He was a unique gift to the cult of Bravgh-Chry.

Although inspired, the travelers didn't follow Harris, the Pilot. Out of respect, they left him to wander.

The first leg of the circuit was complete. Finding Harris was no simple task, and it was finished. That night, the travelers agreed, they would find the plateau where Brisbane's guardian first pointed out Alta Montane's faint light in the sky.

Between one another, as Harris disappeared and his steps faded, they rehashed the old tale of young Brisbane looking outward and inward simultaneously, seeing for the first time. The Pilot was penultimate. The plateau was the crown of their pilgrimage.

# WASP WING

She searched the frozen windowpane, clearing frost with her arm, but she found no reflection that gray morning. The cabin, hidden in the forest, had no other mirrors. She turned to a bare room, austere like the home of woodsmen in fairy tales. There was a bed where the couple had slept and a bed their children had shared. The quilts were handmade. A fireplace dominated one wall of the domicile. A homespun rug covered the floor. Cabinets housed an assortment of utensils and stoppered bottles of tonic. There were two windows.

Outside, a trail led from the door into the woods, a dirt trace that, after miles, intersected with one of the state routes. She tried to recall the number. Was it 784? There were so few signs.

The frozen window meant she couldn't see herself that morning, and the prospect of being blind to her metamorphosis was tragic. Witnessing the beauty of the changing would lessen the agony that scissored her nerves and wrenched her bones. It was the pain of vivisection, of primitive surgeries. Lack of sleep did not help. She did her best to sleep on her stomach, but sleep came only in rapid fits. If she was not so anchored, so devoted, the agony would wreck her mind.

She reached to her back and stroked the protrusions at her shoulders. The skin was flayed, hot with infection, and the wing tips that emerged brought excruciating pain when moved. When the wings shifted (only eight inches had surfaced while the rest waited beneath skin) her spine twisted with the burden.

At the foot of the children's bed, she went to her knees in imitation of prayer. The agony was enough to leave her unconscious, but she ground her teeth in defiance. She placed her ear against a floorboard. The buzzing reached her, then a familiar stench, and then a familiar gravity that gripped her limbs. Ever since the first night, she was pulled. She closed her eyes in a sublime, beatific moment. The aura emanated like steam through the floor.

An unwelcome paranoia gripped her.

She opened her eyes and listened. Grimacing, she rose from the floor.

She often heard their voices, just as she had that first night—the pleasant family sitting down to dinner. Now she heard the voices outside the cabin walls. The same voices, the same family. The three boys. The parents.

Had they come back? Had she been delusional all along? Had they simply left and gone away, now to return?

She used their home as her own. No doubt they were furious. The possibility made her tremble.

In the moment before her increasingly fused fingers met the door to open it wide, she dashed the thought. The family wouldn't return. They couldn't.

They were beneath the floor, weren't they? She could count them when in doubt. The couple. The three boys.

They were rotting in the crawlspace. She smelled them.

If she strained, she could peer through the cracks in the floor and see their wasp-covered corpses. She entombed the bodies herself.

How could the family ever return?

*There are no voices outside of those in your head,* she thought.

She drew a breath and calmed herself. After returning to the frozen window, a positive thought blossomed. The night was cold and snowy, but morning sunlight fought the clouds.

A couple hundred yards from the cabin, in the opposite direction of the road, was a small pond brimming with fish. She had visited once before. Ice glazed the pond's surface, but it was brittle. What better mirror than water stretched beneath the high sun? She searched the cabin for a blanket to jacket her body. Great fortitude kept her from blacking out.

———

SHE'D FOUND the driver and his fellows at the counter, running forks over their plates. A waitress stood opposite the three men, a smirk beneath glass eyes, offering coffee. The men declined then asked for something stronger. Their demeanor made her skin crawl, yet she approached.

*Your name? Who are you, girl? What's your name?*

In shy tones, she demurred.

*We don't talk to strangers, gal.*

Conjoined laughter, a noise she loathed.

She spoke to escape the laughter.

"I'm called Dani," she said. "I need a ride from here."

*Called? Who calls you that?*

Her father did—had—but she refused to answer.

As she left the diner, the glassy-eyed waitress frowned and shook her head in warning. Dani stopped, uncertain, but the men swept her through the door. A bell clanged, and the waitress was gone.

The truck, a boxy Ford with wooden slats enclosing the bed, waited in the lot. Dani had little experience with automobiles. Her father, a demon-haunted preacher, shunned them as "devil carriages." A man had offered to sell her father an open-topped motorcar in 1913, the year before war, but her old man damned him. Preacher had a mare in the barn, he said, and God gave Preacher legs to move about. Isn't that enough?

The flash of that open-topped motorcar, grimy as it was, stuck with Dani. She dreamed about it. The opportunity to ride in the truck, therefore, even with three lecherous men, was alluring. This was her time of rebellion, after all.

How better to continually damn her father?

Once the engine was cranked and running, the men, reeking of body odor and tobacco, crowded into the cab. They insisted Dani ride up front rather than in the bed with straw and crates. Much too cold, they said. They would keep her warm and snug.

The truck took to the road shakily. Rows of brick buildings disappeared, then the houses and yards passed, and then a maw of forest ate the highway.

The men passed Dani back and forth on their laps (even the devil-may-care driver made room), rubbing her body against their erections. Despite Dani's protests, their hands explored and groped. She wore a long coat, but the clothes beneath were thin. With clumsy fingers, the men loosened buttons.

Finally, the truck stopped. The road was dark and shadowy, lined with bare trees and brown-gray undergrowth.

Dani fought back. She clawed, kicked, and hammered.

She screamed until her lungs were bloody pulp. Bruised, the men relinquished their grips and allowed Dani to flee. They laughed together, watching her go. She ran, dashing lithely between the trees, cutting through the resistant bramble.

Dani looked like a cat, they agreed.

*She's a weird one, all right.*

*Something ain't right in her eyes.*

*Fucked in the head. That's what.*

Eventually, the truck coughed and rolled away.

---

SHE STEPPED onto a blanket of snow that stretched over the field and draped trees. It was heavy snow, the type that clumps and crunches. Sunlight emerged at breaks in the clouds, and the warmth had trees dripping. There was comforting peace in the forest, peace she couldn't find in the cabin, no matter how she tried.

Revulsion and gratitude made strange bedfellows.

The cleft in her soul was confusing. With the blanket carefully avoiding the protrusions at her shoulders, she distanced herself from the cabin. In the light, she examined her hands. In a process that began nights prior, her long, delicate fingers fused together, the skin melding, the nails blackening. The hands were folding in on themselves, thinning without withering the bone. Only the thumbs on each remained mobile. Her fingers formed sharp points. It was grotesque. Nauseating.

Guilt flooded her. Where was her gratitude?

Craning her neck, wincing at the pain, she glanced at her right wing. It was black, hard as bone at the edge, and webbed with membrane thin as cheesecloth. The glint of quicksilver covered it, and when sunlight touched the membrane, a rainbow of oil appeared. It was grotesque but also beautiful.

*Find gratitude in the beauty*, she thought.

The wing was revolting and alluring. How would the wing appear when it fully emerged?

As beautiful as one of Preacher's angel wings.

Regardless of her feelings, metamorphosis was a gift. Had she not bargained for the ability to change?

The Goddess granted her such freedom.

If not for pain, she'd be happy. There would be no question then. There would be no cleft, no ingratitude, no revulsion.

The will of her Goddess meant everything.

She looked to the cabin, uneven on sloped earth. At the left of the porch, bound with a rusted latch, a square door enclosed the crawlspace. She'd discovered the Divine there, behind the door. The Divine, which her father had ranted over, mutilated his mind in fear of, begged on his knees in worship of, finally cursed and abandoned in anger of, was not sought. She had not searched for it. The Divine found her.

She considered walking forward and unlatching the door, but mortal fear kept her distant. She had looked upon the shape only once, and that was enough. It was a form best kept in the abstract, best restrained in the back of thoughts.

How would her father react to seeing the Divine? How would he react to seeing his daughter's metamorphosis?

Preacher would lose his mind. *He'd call me a witch.*

She resigned herself to the task at hand, which was not to admonish her father, or to remember him, but to find a reflection. Under the warmth of the sun, she started toward the tree line at the rear of the cabin.

*Witch.*

The word settled uncomfortably. She had never liked it. Her father, frowning over an open Bible, kept the word on his lips.

*Witch.*

She frowned, too, and it was at pain deeper than her bones.

---

DANI HAD RUN from the truck for several miles. She couldn't reckon the distance, but hours had passed, and she hadn't stopped in that time. The sun moved, early winter twilight settling over the trees.

Two things made her stop. First, she'd arrived at a dirt road. Second, she spied a young boy, bundled against the weather, standing in the road, overturning rocks with a stick in his fist. The boy was lost in play.

Breathlessly, lungs burning cold, Dani approached. Unlike with the men in the truck, she felt no need for caution. She raised her hand to the child, and the boy waved back amicably.

It was dark when she and the boy reached the cabin. The first image of the home nestled in a clearing, smoke enveloping the roof, candles in the windows like Jack-o'-Lantern eyes, pleasant voices and chatter emanating from within, would remain in her mind, because the image was deceptive rather than idyllic. The façade masked what lay below.

These were people like her father. They shared Preacher's sensibilities, his notions, his wickedness.

As they approached, the boy cheerfully leading his guest to dinner, the cabin's front door opened, revealing a tall, broad silhouette and a swath of firelight. Obviously, the boy had a fondness for stray animals, because his father chided him for bringing home yet another. When Dani stepped into the light, her presence made for an odd meeting. The father, a quietly angry, red-faced man, was distant and wary. He searched Dani's eyes.

Reluctantly, he allowed the stray into his home. He kept the boy on the porch, however, and the father whispered angrily at his son.

It was a family of five, a mother, father, and three sons ranging from four to twelve years in age. The mother invited Dani to sit for dinner. The mother did not eat. The elder brothers watched Dani in such a way that she wondered if they would grow to be lecherous men like the truckers.

That night, Dani lay awake on the floor, bundled in a quilt, listening to the family sleep. A thump and rattle from beneath the house stole her attention from the quintet of shallow breaths. Something large moved in the crawlspace. Dani listened more closely, moving aside the bundled sheet she used as a pillow. Through the wood, a low, intense buzzing emanated, the mad chatter of angry insects. Once again, something large shifted its weight. The planks rattled against her cheek. The buzzing grew louder.

Suddenly, the darkness deepened around her, and Dani looked up from the ground, startled. The father stood tall, his stance reminding Dani of her old man. His knees creaked as he knelt.

*Outside*, he whispered.

She followed the man out the front door. The night was blustery, moving her hair about, cutting through the folds of her jacket. Her feet were bare and hard as ice. The father, after closing the door, handed Dani her worn leather shoes.

*You must leave*, he said.

He was so stern in his demeanor, so unmoved, he

reminded Dani of the granite Confederate soldiers she'd admired in town. She found herself attracted to him. She reached for his hand and touched the corded flesh. He looked off into the moonlight but didn't resist. After sliding into her shoes, Dani followed him from the porch.

Once upon the dirt road, he spoke.

*Temptress.*

There was venom in the word. From an inner pocket, the father pulled a Bible. Without opening the pages, he showed it in the silvery light. The book was well worn, the pages marked at close intervals.

*My wife says you're a witch. She can feel it. She says you got a devil in your eyes. You're no better than a wasper. A weird one, aren't you?*

Dani didn't know what to say. The accusation left her detached. She stared, and she was cold.

*Be on your way,* the father said. *You aren't welcome here.*

He left her at the road. In the distance, Dani spotted candles in the windows, and she saw four faces hooded by curtains.

---

SNOW HID the trail that led to the pond. She was not so familiar with the land that she could do without a path, so she took a meandering route, winding between trees, looking less at the ground and more at the familiar patches of forest. The pond wasn't far. As she walked, keeping her spine still as possible, a twin memory, although years apart, came to her. She could not explain why the memories were conjoined, but the episodes never returned to her separately anymore.

She crunched through the snow, pushing aside limbs,

lost in thought. The sun was pleasingly warm. The trees dripped.

Memory one:

Her father, a shape and voice in her bedroom, woke her from a dream. She couldn't recall the dream, but she remembered the jarring cut from lucid sleep to fogged reality. She recalled the shape and voice, the genuine concern Preacher conveyed, which was rare.

He found her altar, he said, the patch of forest she cleared by hand, the animal bones so intricately placed, the collection of wasp nests, the mismatched teeth, a pile of gray ash where incense and forest herbs burned. Preacher was not angry. He had failed her, he admitted.

How could he be so foolish? How could she?

Memory two:

Overlaying this recollection was another. The Goddess, the mother below the sleeping cabin, taught her to utilize shadows. Hurt and eager, Dani learned quickly. She entered the cabin as subtle as a breath, without disturbing the sleeping couple or their children. There were no candle flames, and the fire burned low. She carved shapes from the shadows, and she brought the shapes to their feet. She approached the beds like Preacher once approached her own. Shadows moved over the boys. Shadows moved over the mother and father.

Below her feet, the Goddess shifted her bulk, and her wing pushed against the floor. Her barb stabbed the mud. The Goddess trilled with excitement.

In her hands, Dani held honeycombed nests of myriad shapes and sizes, stolen from holes in the crawlspace. She lay the nests about the boys' necks, and she stuffed nests into their mouths, creating ghastly smiles. She covered the faces of the mother and father, placing nests on their eyelids. With shadows coating their bodies, no one awoke, not until the thin-waisted Goddess scuttled and awakened her children.

Dani looked back to where she pocked the virgin snow, then she looked ahead to the shimmer of sun and ice. Steam snaked over the pond. Despite the pain, she smiled. The thought of her reflection brought an exhilarating fear. She felt alive.

She was grateful.

---

WHEN THE FATHER had returned to the cabin and firelight shrank from the windows, Dani moved from her perch on the road. She could not bring herself to obey the man. More than that, something called to her, pulled her with a whisper. Behind the wind, there was a palpable thrumming in the air, the beating of wings, emanating from the crawl-space. Bundled, Dani walked gingerly over the grass, arms crossed atop her stomach. The icy wind sliced in, rattling shingles on the cabin roof. One shingle, held with a single nail, lifted and fell rhythmically. A weathervane, somewhere near but hidden in darkness, creaked.

Had Dani not experienced a similar beckoning before? Of course, she was a child then, new to the Veil. With a child's eagerness and ignorance, she peered beyond. That was in the forest when wild things grew over her altar. On that night, a similar pulsing gravity had called her from sleep. She'd gone and retreated, however, too soon. Her mind was too fragile for the sight awaiting her. Dani glimpsed it only briefly.

The wing, she remembered, was rumpled like the skin of a vulture claw. Foolish of the opportunity, she witnessed no more.

Tonight was a new opportunity, a second chance. No

longer a child, Dani was ready to receive the gift of sight. How would the vision alter her? she wondered.

With mixed emotion, Dani ran her hands over the cabin's stone foundation. To the side of the porch, her palms left cold rock and patted a wooden door. Her heart quickened. She found the latch, gritty with rust. She pushed the door inward.

The thick stench of mildew and mold roiled from the cabin's underbelly. The air was thick, warmer than the night, and windless. Dani reached through the threshold and planted her hands against a skin of mud. She ducked her head and entered. From mud to the floor above, the space was only two feet high, less when the ground raised in mounds. With the door open, weak moonlight reached inside. From above, firelight pierced cracks in the floorboards, casting pinstripes of orange. The light was enough to keep the crawlspace from having the blackness of a cave, but it was not enough to subdue Dani's anxiety.

*You're not a child anymore*, she scolded, but her fear didn't bow to the rebuke.

The feeling swelled in her chest, and then it became a copper flavor at the rear of her tongue.

*A second chance*, she reminded herself. *You were foolish before.*

The clatter of wasp wings reminded her that she was not alone. She crawled farther. Wasn't it odd for wasps to be so active in winter, to be awake? Regardless, she didn't fear their sting. That was part of the beckoning, a promise of safety from the poisonous barbs. Indeed, even as her groping hands fell into holes and crushed nests, the wasps avoided her touch. Although they sounded angry, they kept distant.

Perhaps it was the pressure of the space and wind, maybe it was more, but the door slammed shut, cutting away moonlight. Only the slats of light from above remained. Dani was nauseous and unwilling, as if she'd awakened from a spell of sleepwalking. Paralysis snaked through her limbs, slowing her advance. She craned her neck, peering into one of the far corners.

The Goddess revealed a shape. What she was before, or what she would be after, Dani could not say, but her current form was that of a wasp. The insect was inconceivably large, filling the space from mud to floor. The massive wings tottered. The triangular head and swollen hindquarters moved in opposite directions, hinged by a minute waist. Floorboards shuddered at the disturbance.

The Goddess, patient with ages, peered inside.

Dani found no shame in the loosening of her bowels.

*Witch.*

Her father's voice. The voice, too, of the man in the cabin above. Her voice, too, wrapping the ugly little word.

*Priestess,* the Goddess corrected.

Watching the dark figure, she felt a completeness she never knew before. The connection was overwhelming.

*Priestess,* Dani thought.

The wasp did not move to attack her, although it rattled closer. The barb probed mud, carving a trench.

The Goddess, like Dani, approved the nomenclature.

———

PREACHER, she reflected, once murdered a black feline with a shovel. When he offered reason, he was terse.

*The devil's brood,* Preacher said, his eyes distant, plumbing memories.

He smeared blood in a patch of weeds by the front lawn, cleaning the shovel. He threw the cat's broken body into a fast-flowing creek, recently engorged by a downpour.

Dani had captured the animal in the woods as a kitten, a stray, and she nursed it to robust health. The cat was hidden until now.

Impudently, she asked, *How does killing it make you any better?*

*Who's worse?* said Preacher. *The murderer of the body? Or the murderer of the soul?*

He was, she realized, a heinous ogre.

Preacher hurt her so deeply and so often that the grudge in her heart would not accept his death, drawn out and agonizing as it was, as sufficient payment. His suffering was over. She wished, and not even the Goddess could grant this, that she could prolong his suffering, draw up his ghost with cat blood and let him watch the metamorphosis through her eyes.

She wanted to torment the man. She wanted to tell him that she never destroyed the altar, nor did he.

Was her father watching? He would say so, but she figured he remained in the coffin, a tangle of mold-encrusted bones.

She pressed through remnants of brown cattails and brittle weed stalks taller than the snow, making her way to the pond. As she approached, she shed the blanket. The garment fell into a crown at her heels. Above, clouds dispersed, and the sun was bright and large.

Dani felt like a basking cat.

*The devil's brood*, her father said.

*Why?*

*Vessels,* he said. *God knows what cats carry. Spirits. Worse.*

*Can people change into cats?*

He scoffed. It was amazing how selective he was in his superstitions.

*Fairy tales,* Preacher muttered.

She dashed the thin coating of ice with a stone. Snow

crunched as she knelt. She moved her face over the rippling water. The edge of wasp wings poked over her shoulders. Her hands were blackening, as was the sclera of her left eye. She stayed in that position for much of the morning. With concentration, focusing on the drifting shards of ice and the squirming minnows drawn to sunlight, her hand transformed and became human again. Inkiness swirled and receded from her eye. The wings remained. She flexed her fingers.

Painful as it was, and revolting as it appeared, it was a metamorphosis she would learn to command.

# SCOURGE OF THE FLESH DEVIL: A TALE OF FRANKENSTEIN

I t was the last winter he would see in Karlsbadt. A deep freeze settled in the foothills, leaving islands of ice in the river, and leaving the many ponds through the countryside frozen a foot deep. Snow fell, obscuring the distant mountains with gray.

The glacial air shocked his lungs. An argument with his wife drove him from the warmth of his bed that morning. He told her that he was going to work early, which was untrue. He simply wanted a walk to clear his mind of last night's wine and his wife's nagging. At the door, she told him to forget about returning home that evening.

The road was frozen and craggy. The clustered buildings of Karlsbadt—a few of painted brick, most of knotted wood—billowed steam and smoke at their rooftops. With two hours remaining until he needed to be at work in the stables, he turned from the road and walked into the forest.

Two inches of snow covered the ground—heavy, wet snow that made a satisfying crunch under his boots. Trees drooped. The forest was silent of birds and animals. He walked into the hush, letting his anger drain away. Finding a trail through the trees, pristine save for the occasional deer print, he walked an hour before an old warning, relayed to him by his father, surfaced in his mind.

He was in the Baron's Forest.

He stopped and glanced at the trees.

*No traveler returns alive*, he thought.

That's what parents told children in Karlsbadt. The Baron's Forest was full of ghosts, with a fairy circle hidden at its heart. Degenerate, fleshless men walked its copious graveyards. There were as many stories as there were generations in the village. The truth was that the forest was old, and the Barons Karlsbadt, whose stone chateau waited behind a garden of trees, were a reclusive family of means who built the village and saw to its care. Sometimes their carriages were spotted on the road, but seeing the family was rare.

Personally, he had never seen a Karlsbadt.

Curiosity took hold, so he chanced tardiness at the stables and continued onward. Despite a full life in the barony, he had never seen the Baron's home. He was too close to allow the opportunity to fall away. His wife boasted about visiting the chateau as a child, about waiting in a wagon outside the front gates while her mother went inside and asked for work.

Thousands of ancient trees fortified the estate. The trail sloped through a grove.

*They must maintain a forester*, he thought, peering around as he labored upward.

Not only was brush cleared between the trees, the branches and trunks held decorations. At the mouth of the grove, crosses, two atop one another, were nailed into the bark of an age-old birch. The decoration became less Christian and more pagan as he entered. Wooden chimes dangled from the trees, knocking, catching snow and wind.

*Heathens,* he thought. *What would Parson Bateman say about all this?*

Through the gnarled branches, he saw puffs of smoke. Then he spotted a rooftop and eaves, as the sprawling chateau came into view. A fence did not guard the home. He walked freely onto the grounds, feeling small as he approached the immense structure.

*Nobility is supposed to inspire deference*, his father once told him. Now he saw how they achieved it. He thought of his own home and his ugly wife inside it, and of his daughter, already widowed and ashamed. His was a thatched roof, and his walls were weak as planks.

*I'm a small man*, he thought, *quite small.*

There was more to the home than immensity. An air hung about the structure, from its pointed towers to its weather-faded brick and all the way down into the frozen water surrounding its base. The feeling struck him as odd, even frightening. The home did not feel lived-in. The air was decayed. When one finally accepted the size of the home, other details, less striking but more telling, appeared. Vines, dead with winter, consumed the walls like spider webs, invading the highest windows. Briar and brown grass choked the gardens, spilling onto a rutted driveway. Atop the moat lay a pile of furniture: carved tables, chairs cushioned with velvet, shelves broken into kindling.

He walked to the frozen artery of water. The tossed furniture left scratches in the ice. He wondered how much of the furniture he could salvage. Putting one foot against the freeze, he tested its resilience. The ice held without a groan of complaint. He walked out and picked a chair with red velvet from the pile.

*What'll the wife think now*, he thought. He wondered how

quickly she'd say sorry when he brought this home. *A chair good enough for the Baron, at least at one time.*

*How'd you come by something so lovely?*

*Wouldn't you like to know, dear?*

*Come home, indeed,* she'd say. *My smart, loving man.*

He was content to leave for home, but an image in the ice stopped him. He looked through one of his footprints.

Something moved in the water below.

After setting aside the chair, he knelt and cleared snow from the surface. Certainly, something moved in the water, although the image was too fogged to see clearly.

*A fish,* he thought. *An immense fish.*

The thing below saw him, too. It moved closer to the surface.

Was it gulping for air? Was it scratching at the ice? The hand, although frozen blue, looked human.

"My God," he whispered.

The thing scratched at the handprint he left on the moat. A distinct, terrified face formed. There was a man beneath the ice. No, it was not a man. Terror lodged in his throat. A living corpse pushed against the ice. The face was skeletal, with rotten ribbons of flesh, white as snow in the water, floating on the bones. When the thing quit its struggle, it sank into the sludge.

A tangle of sounds—a hairline crack spreading in the ice, the snarl of a torch flame, the grumble of a man trying to speak—stole his attention. He looked up.

There was a figure atop the ice as well as beneath it. Although wrapped cloth concealed the body, the exposed face was rotten and skeletal like the one below. In fact, the faces were strikingly similar. Tendons stretched tautly when the thing's mouth opened.

Looking up at the approaching figure, he disgorged a

scream that, to the villagers awakening in town, sounded curiously like the shriek of a young woman.

———————

WHEN THE TAVERN opened for lunch, Paul was on the wrong side of town, smoking a cigarette and thinking, as was his habit lately, of Maria. The bell pealed, cutting through avenues and across the smoke-enveloped rooftops of Karlsbadt. How proper that a church bell interrupted his imagination, dashed his vivid and lewd image of the parson's daughter. Paul counted the bell's rings. At the twelfth note, he flung his cigarette into the snow and started toward work.

Wind cut into his thin coat and hardened his features.

*Two more hours of snow*, he thought, *and the village will be buried*. Measuring the imprint of his shoe, he counted five inches. Whether an inch or three feet, snow didn't close the tavern. In fact, the worse the weather, the more men flocked to the warm, beer-stinking abode. Little work could be done on a day like this, and men quickly tired of wives and children.

*I wish I could be home*, Paul thought, *with Maria by the fire, on a blanket spread before the heat. She would be ready and willing.* He thought back three nights to when he first kissed her— he'd never experienced such a thrill through his bones. *Maybe she'll visit today*, he thought. *But, then again, parsons' daughters do not visit taverns. Not lightly.*

He let out a sigh that hinted at his adolescence. Despite his broad shoulders, his dark eyes full of other people's laundry, and his assured, arrogant countenance, Paul was only eighteen years old.

The tavern door was shut tight against the storm. Oil lamps burned in the windows and the chimney coughed smoke. After kicking snow from his shoes, Paul opened the door and dashed inside. A lance of arctic wind escaped the fissure, chilling the tables and bending flames.

Michael stood behind the bar, hands against the scarred oak, in his usual attire: sleeves rolled to his elbows, collar down, leather apron across his chest, towel balanced on his shoulder. Of his thinning hair only a smattering of curls remained, one of which, an island, lay against the peak of his forehead.

"What kept you?" he asked.

His smile was deceptive. Strangers thought the look an amused one. Those accustomed to Michael realized it was the only way he knew how to express anger. He only smiled when he was mad.

Paul chanced a look around the room. One man, Neil Cummings, sat at a table near the fire. With his head down and a mug of warm beer in his fist, he was a mix of shadows, part of the decoration. Neil had had two glasses of beer every afternoon since Paul was employed.

"The storm kept me, sir. I wasn't prepared for it this morning."

Michael grunted, staring into Paul until the boy looked away. "Get an apron on," he said.

"You got last night's dishes to worry about."

When Paul split the batwing doors and stepped into the backroom, he saw that Georgie was at the sink, an apron tied at her waist, hands groping in a mountain of suds. She didn't disguise the apologetic look on her face.

"I tried," she said.

Paul dipped his head and laughed. After tying on his apron, he joined her.

"Tried what exactly?"

"To cover for you." She nodded at a pile of dishes, waiting to be dried.

"The sweetest girl in town," he said. He lifted a towel from the shelf.

"The hell I am. It wouldn't be much of a place to work if it were Michael and me tackling those drunkards. And you, in case you ain't noticed, are wearing on his nerves. He already thinks you're full of yourself. Just give him a good reason."

"I don't think so," Paul said. "He likes me more than you do."

"Well, I like you more than I like him, so don't get cut loose on me."

Paul smiled.

Georgie's cheeks colored. She turned her eyes to the bubbles. Despite her manner, which was often cold as carved marble, Georgie was a complex soul. She had thick, raven hair that she piled in a loose bun atop her head, allowing strands to hang down and tickle her ears. Her skin was not fair but tanned. There was nothing fair about her looks, even her eyes had a touch of onyx in them.

Paul had learned quite a bit about her in the past year. Her father, who sauntered into the tavern expecting free draughts of wine, worked at the livery stable and sold firewood for a living. He was a miserable man, unhappy but kind, who managed to love and ignore his daughter simultaneously. Georgie, twenty-six, was married to a soldier briefly. The man had either died, became a prisoner in the Balkans, or run off—the story depended on Georgie's mood. Regardless, she counted herself a single woman, thankfully childless but dreadfully lonely

"Why so glum?" Paul asked, placing dry dishes on the shelf above the sink.

"My mother kicked my father out this morning. He left early. Before work I stopped at the stables. Dirk said he hadn't shown up yet. I said he left two hours early. I'm afraid he's run off."

Paul didn't know what to say. He thought, however, of the shriek he heard from the forest this morning, and he shuddered. The cutting noise had pulled him from sleep.

Out front, Michael slammed a mug against the counter and hurried toward the door. Wind roared inward. There was commotion in the street, people gathering.

Paul and Georgie pushed through the batwing doors, hands and arms damp, aprons their only defense against the cold. They joined Michael under the porch awning. Neil Cummings joined, too. Indeed, a crowd formed in the street. A man was at the center of it, pulling a sled with a rope over his shoulder. His cargo was a rough pine box, oblong and coated with snow. He called for any man who could point him to the Baron.

*This will be a day of endings*, Paul thought.

The words, forming unconsciously, gave him pause. He shook his head clear, but intuition remained. He thought of the scream and Georgie's missing father.

"The Baron," the man shouted. "Show me the road to the Baron!"

---

WHEN THEY COMMITTED SUICIDE, the Swede told him, they were buried in the bog. It wasn't Christian to plant a Hell-bound soul in consecrated earth, and no man of morals would argue otherwise. Dutch was inclined to agree. Although not a man of morals (he'd be buried in the bog if he stuck around), he recognized opportunity. And this opportunity, if carried out under the cover of night, was golden. Dirty work, yes, but profitable.

Dutch learned two vital pieces of information from the

Swede. First, the bog bodies, smothered in the peat, mummified over time, like the Egyptians but without the fine tombs and jewels. Occasionally, the corpses resurfaced, poking a leathery arm or leg from the muck. Wild dogs then plundered the graves, a fit ending for men and women who so despised God that they took their own lives. The Swede bragged that his own pup shat a couple fingers on his back porch once.

*Still got 'em on the mantle*, he said, *straight outta Hell.*

*I'm no better than a stray dog,* Dutch reasoned, with a touch of pride. *We're both ghouls.*

The second fact relayed by the Swede spoke directly to Dutch's heart. Down in Germany, in a backwater settlement called Karlsbadt, there was a baron scientist who had an interest in mummification.

*He's buying*, the Swede said, *any mummified cadaver he can get his hands on. Conducting experiments.*

Dutch was intrigued. *How came you by this information?*

The Swede smiled. *Let's say I knew him the first time he was run out by the Germans.*

*Fine, let's say that.*

*Fine. Let's say I was in business with him.*

*How so?*

*I dug graves. He bought 'em fresh and warm from the noose, I'll have you know.*

*Paid a pretty penny?*

*It ain't legal, is it? What do you think?*

Cudgels in hand, the men headed for the wetlands. The first corpse they hauled from the muck was ill preserved.

*Too much water in this one*, the Swede observed.

Indeed, the corpse, a woman with hair the consistency of weeds around her shattered crown, was a delicate bag of mud and slop. The cudgels cut through her like wet paper. Dutch tried to shove her back beneath the peat, but he only got her shoulders under, leaving the screaming mouth and skeletal jaws exposed.

*The dogs will take care of her*, Dutch thought, wiping the sweat of hard labor from his brow. Twice he'd heard dogs moving in the underbrush. Veteran to the wetlands, they waited for dinner.

As the night dragged, Dutch lost his patience and confidence in the Swede. Knowing precisely how his fits of rage landed him in trouble, he feigned calmness. He smoothed the tremble in his hands, then he became more gracious with the Swede, referring to him as *my friend.* Dutch hid rage behind a veil of kindness. The habit served him well.

Thankfully for he and the Swede, the second body their trawl uncovered was hard as a fossil.

*My friend, we've done it*, he said, and for a moment his anger withered.

This corpse was older than the first, its brown, leathery face closed and peaceful, its bones without trauma.

*It's like he went for a swim and never came up*, said the Swede. *I bet he's a thousand years old.*

*How would you know that?* Dutch's hands twitched.

The Swede, affronted, replied, *I'm in the business. Who got you out here in the first place?*

Dutch stabbed the Swede thirteen times in the face, neck, and chest, and then beat his brains to mush with the cudgel. Afterwards, as he slid his friend into the peat, he felt guilt for not preserving the skull. He cursed himself. He could've sold the brain, feeble as it was, along with the bog mummy.

*Karlsbadt*, Dutch thought, trying to focus.

He pulled the mummified corpse onto an island of dry grass and collected himself.

*Karlsbadt.*

---

"I HAVE BEEN ENTRUSTED," the parson said. He stopped, looking up from the snowy ground for the first time since crossing his doorstep, and he scanned the crowd amassed in the thoroughfare. "Good God in Luther's lavatory," he said. "What in the Hell is all this?"

Maria looked into the crowd and spotted the cause of excitement. A crooked little man with a rope over his shoulder, and a sled at the end of the rope, asked questions from a group of three. Michael, Paul's employer, was among the three.

Her father, Parson Bateman, with a shock of gray hair that vanity kept uncovered in winter, didn't wait for an answer. He used his remarkably loud voice to clear a path.

"What is this?" he asked. "What is all this?"

The crowd's murmuring thinned to whispers, and even the crooked man turned his attention to the gaunt parson.

Maria, protected under a coat and tightly wrapped shawl, spotted Paul on the tavern steps, his arms crossed, leaning against a rail. At his elbow stood Georgie.

*She's unclean*, her father said. He spoke the word—next to atheist, his favorite slur—like it was poisonous. *You'll be unclean if you hang around that young man who works beside her.*

*Paul is different. He's smart, father. He has a curious view of things.*

*Curious? Does that mean he's an atheist?*

*I don't think so.*

*Personally, I've never seen the wretch in church. He's the reason pews gather dust.*

*There are other churches, father.*

*I don't want to see you with him. Not ever. Nor at that dreadful tavern.*

Maria sympathized with her father's view of Georgie, but he couldn't be more wrong about Paul. As she snuck around the crowd, snippets of the odd conversation reached her.

"What's in the box?" her father demanded. As usual, he pushed other men aside and took control.

"I say, it ain't none of your concern."

"The Baron is an important part of our town."

"Good," the crooked man said curtly. "Point out his road."

"I say, first you tell what's in the box. If I didn't know better, I'd say it was a coffin box."

"Grab him," someone in the crowd said.

"We'll take his head off if he wants to play games," said another.

"I don't mean a damn harm to a single one of you. This box is for the Baron, and what's inside belongs to him and him alone."

"Paul?" Maria said.

She reached the steps without Paul noticing. Georgie, however, had watched every step of her approach. She turned away, wearing a sneer.

"Maria!"

Paul clambered down the steps, stopping short of taking Maria into his arms. Rather than an embrace, he chanced a look at her father, who was still flustered and preoccupied.

Maria smiled. Beneath her coat, she wore a blouse with such a low cut that, had her father known, he would've branded her with an iron. She wanted to go inside, remove the coat, and allow Paul to look upon her. She feared God as much as a parson's daughter could, but she felt strong lust for Paul, and the feeling became harder and harder to resist. The right circumstances, in her father's view, would turn her Hellbound.

"You're not wearing a coat," she said, "you must be freezing."

Indeed, Paul's unbuttoned sleeves hung loosely around his wrists. His leather apron was little protection. Maria grabbed his cold hand.

"It's inside," Paul said. "All this caught my attention. And yours, too." He winked. "And your father's, I see."

"You hear."

"I hear."

"Let's step inside," Maria said.

She was following Paul up the steps when carriage wheels and horses crunching snow grabbed everyone's attention.

Even the argument between the parson and the crooked man ceased. A phrase of the parson's hung in the air, echoing curiously around the frozen town.

"Let's say I speak for the Baron!"

The driver who stepped from the carriage was so bundled and wrapped in cloth that his face, his entire body, was hidden from view. He was a gigantic man. His gait was odd and awkward. Only his dark, wet eyes and frosted clouds of breath emerged. He turned his back on the crowd and opened the carriage door.

The man inside was not so hidden. He stepped out with the trained grace of a nobleman. He was a man of small stature, naturally thin, with striking features—an aquiline nose, gaunt cheeks, wary but deeply intelligent eyes. His posture, and the lift of his chin, spoke arrogance. He was a man of little toleration, a man who cut through life like wind. He raised his hands, both cloaked in leather.

"Now," he said smoothly, "who again speaks for me here?"

The parson, unaccustomed to being outshined, scoffed.

The Baron's eyes picked him from the crowd.

"Is it you?" he asked.

With the bulky driver at his side, the Baron strode forward.

Maria looked at Paul. Her father, for all his learning, was a dense and stupid man.

"I am Parson Bateman."

"Noted. And who are you?" The Baron looked at the crooked man.

With eyes to the ground, he said, "My name's Dutch."

"Allow me to enlighten you, Parson. You do not, and will never, in fact, speak for me."

"Yes, sir," the parson said tightly.

"The rest of you men disperse," the Baron said. "This is my business. It is none of your own. Help the gentleman with his box," he told the driver.

Dutch smiled, revealing a broken line of teeth.

"Aye, friend," he said. "I'm obliged."

"Get into the carriage," the Baron ordered.

The driver, with little effort, picked the pine box from the man's sled.

When the carriage doors were closed, Bateman aired his opinion of the matter.

"That isn't the Baron I know. In fact, I'd venture that isn't the Baron at all."

Maria released Paul's hand just before the gaze of her father fell on her.

The black carriage made a wide turn, breaking a path through the snow, and headed toward the hills.

---

FROM WITHIN THE darkness of the funereal carriage, Dutch looked upon the Baron with smug satisfaction. The ride was slow, the horses struggling on an incline slick with snow. The driver cracked a whip. The wheels, wrapped in chains, groaned. Trees pressed against the narrowing path, scraping at the doors on either side.

"Maybe my manners aren't adequate, friend, but let's say we talk business."

The Baron smiled. "You have manners? I didn't notice."

"To be in your carriage, sir, I must. You wouldn't take any vagabond off the road, would you?"

"I would. In fact, I did. What are you looking to sell?"

Dutch managed his anger, hiding it deeply.

"A dear friend of mine up north said he had word that you, friend, well… that you was buyin' dead bodies for an experiment. He said you're a man of science."

"You don't mean to tell me you traveled all the way here with a rotting corpse in a box, do you?" The Baron scoffed.

"No, I don't mean that. My friend—"

"—And what, pray tell, happened to this friend?"

"Detained. It is a dangerous business, after all."

"I see. Go on."

"My friend said you was studying mummies."

"The process of mummification, yes."

"Good. 'Cause that's what I got in the box. It's from the bog, friend. It's real old. My friend says a thousand years, but that'd make him a caveman or something, wouldn't it?"

The Baron smirked. "We'll see," he said.

After a moment of silence, Dutch went on. "Here go my manners again, but let's say we talk money. How much would you pay for something along those lines, say it was authentic?"

"I'll give you a price after I examine it."

"Fair enough, friend," Dutch said. "You strike me as a fair man twice over. How does one get to be a baron, anyhow?" He guffawed.

Unamused, the Baron turned his eyes to the rectangular window in the carriage door.

*Maybe you just take it*, Dutch thought. He imagined himself with fine clothes and a driver. *All you got to do is smirk when people try to talk to you, and then you order them around when you want something.*

The Baron reminded him of a prison guard he knew, equally aloof, equally arrogant.

The carriage jolted to a stop. Dutch opened his door and stepped out into the bitter cold. His shoes were wet, and his feet ached—he was afraid he'd freeze if he remained outside. The Baron waited for the driver's aid, which came slowly and without a word.

Dutch was disappointed to look upon the sprawling battlements of the Baron's home. The structure looked unattended, even abandoned. Debris, and the smoldering ashes of a fire, littered the moat. The ice was open where the fire burned.

The driver led the way across a stone bridge. He carried the pine box, a weight Dutch could barely pull on a sled, under his arm like a bundle of twigs. The Baron followed, rubbing at one of his gloved hands.

Dutch was a man of few emotions. He experienced lust and anger but few things between. Standing atop the bridge, with the tall forest framed over his shoulders, he experienced a rare feeling. Emotions complicated his mind, tightened his nerves into a coil.

*I'm no child*, he thought.

He spat on cold stone. Looking upon the scars of a once fine chateau, he felt ghosts in the air. Fear reached deep inside. He trailed the Baron into the shadowed front hall. He tried his damnedest, but anger didn't replace fear.

---

IN GARB that betrayed his privileged roots, he had fled into the forest with his creations. Both creatures were dear to him. How could he leave them behind? The Burgomaster was fool enough to have them burned to shards of bone and ash, to destroy them totally. Were they not living beings? Could they not breathe, walk, and even think?

The creatures were no more than offal vomited from the bowels of Satan, the Burgomaster had said, brandishing a torch. They were fiends of dead flesh, abominations in God's house. And their creator was even more of an offense. His actions, his presumptions, marked him an evil man. He was a devil in the flesh.

Men had burned his ancestral home, and with the home his equipment, his notes, the work of a lifetime. He had burned his hands to save what he could. The scars ruined his dexterity, rendering him incapable of performing future surgeries. His assistant, a dedicated soul, breathed in too much smoke in his effort to salvage what remained. He had slumped into the flames, cooking without screams. The two things dearest to him were spared the torch. They had hidden in the forest that night, like cowering children with an invasion afoot. He had found them and coaxed them from their shelter.

Strong, hardy, and fast, they blazed a trail through the dark woods—a forest he had explored thoroughly as a boy. He had discovered his intellect here, like Thoreau at Walden Pond, and now it was a means of escape for what that intellect reaped. His mind had uncovered wonderful things. His discoveries cheated death. In another time, he would be a god. Here and now, however, he was a heretic, dabbling in a realm to which he didn't belong. Here, he was running through a midnight forest, trying to do nothing more than save his neck.

There was no moon that night. Only thrashing and breathing and, occasionally, a tangle of distant voices reached him. The voices grew fainter until they ceased. By morning, the chase was over. Ruined and scarred, he had escaped.

His creations followed through the woods and along the occasional road. Like feeble-minded children, the creatures competed for his attention and affection. While he slept, they tried to stand guard, watching the woods until fatigue became too much. As they travelled, he taught them language, and this, too, became a competition. In these lessons, he found he'd made a mistake with the vocal cords of the larger of the two, the one he named Christopher. The throat and its inner workings had deteriorated to mush. No matter how hard Christopher tried to mouth words, he managed little more than clogged, foul smelling groans. The smaller of the two, whom he christened David, learned to speak in a garbled tongue.

Sitting at the edge of their camp, watching his sleeping brother with a smirk, David could say *good morning* quite clearly.

Deterioration was a fault with both creatures. Their flesh rotted and fell away. To protect them from passersby, he ripped his jacket into twin cowls to hide their faces. A slimy film developed on their skin, and the liquid smelled worse than the split belly of a dead pig.

Christopher and David were aware of the changes. One morning, he found them with their hands in a stream, scrubbing the film from their wrists and forearms, gasping when a ribbon of flesh fell from Christopher's arm.

David had approached him that night when Christopher, propped against a tree, closed his eyes to sleep.

"Help us," David said. "We're dying."

He had created life, now he was determined to preserve the casing that held the spark.

Emaciated, a bag of bones, he followed a southern trail to a settlement carved in the foothills called Karlsbadt. There, with Christopher and David in tow, he found a way to continue his experiments.

---

AFTER THE CARRIAGE disappeared into the tree line, Paul reentered the tavern. Warmth wrapped his body. Georgie waited at the bar. Michael was cleaning tables.

"What'd that little man call himself?" Paul asked.

Pastor Bateman had pulled Maria from his side with a sneer of contempt, and Paul needed distraction to keep anger at bay. Bateman looked down his nose like he believed Paul meant harm to his daughter. Paul was tempted to speak his mind as the pastor stomped off, arm locked with Maria's, but he'd found the strength to keep his mouth sealed.

Regardless, he liked that the Baron made a fool out of Bateman in front of parishioners. He'd never seen Maria's father take a seat to a man more willful than he.

*Enemy of my enemy,* he thought.

Without turning, Michael answered Paul's question, "Dutch or some such tripe."

Dutch was a nasty, ugly man with a twisted back and slanted, unshaven face. He looked criminal. He was kindling, however, in the grand scheme of things. The

Baron was the one who really grabbed Paul's attention. Paul wanted to admire him, but a voice in his mind spoke caution. Confused, he walked to the fireplace and extended his hands to the heat. His bones thawed.

"Either of you seen the Baron before today?"

Michael said nothing. He moved to another table and slapped down the rag.

Georgie shrugged. "Why are you so curious?" she asked.

"Bateman said that man wasn't the Baron. He acted like he knew."

"Doesn't he always?" Georgie smiled. "It doesn't look like he approves of you either."

"Oh, you noticed? I thought he treated me like an old friend."

"By his standards, he did."

"He sure likes to turn the old screw, I'll say that." Michael stepped forward with the soiled rag on his shoulder. "To answer your question, I ain't seen one of the barons in all my years. And I've been right here. Bateman was full of piss and wind when he said that. If I ain't seen 'em, Bateman sure as Hell ain't. A bag of hot air, he is. But the whole blasted thing is odd, I'll admit. You catch a look at the box he had? That fellah Dutch?"

"It looked like a coffin," Georgie said.

"Aye, it did." Michael leaned on the bar. He lowered his voice. "I chanced a look," he said, "when they was arguin'." He placed his hand flat on the counter. "I'm steady. I haven't drunk anything since last night. Attest to it."

"Me?" Paul asked. Containing his smile, he sniffed the air around Michael's head. "Sure, you're sober as a schoolmarm."

"Well, get to it. What'd you see?" Georgie asked.

"A bloody corpse," he whispered.

"Aw, go on," Paul said. Then, "You're serious, aren't you?" He looked at Georgie. "He's serious."

Michael nodded at his prostrate hand. "Steady as stone," he said. "You attested. And speakin' of that problem, Georgie dear, get a cheap bottle off the rack. A bloody corpse," he repeated. "The man was draggin' about a bloody corpse."

As Georgie poured a drink, Paul turned and walked to the backroom where the morning dishes waited.

"Why would a man pull a corpse around?" Georgie, incredulous, asked.

Michael threw back a drink. He grunted. A hundred years prior and he would've blurted the magic word: witchcraft. People were embarrassed to go that far now, although the feeling remained.

*A bloody corpse*, Paul thought. Behind him, the batwing doors creaked and stilled. An insane idea occurred to him as he reached into the flat, cold suds. *That could've been Georgie's father in the box. Christ on the Cross. Dutch could've been hauling about a murdered man.*

Paul disagreed with Michael about Bateman's observation. Whether he was the Baron or not, there was something very wrong with the gloved man who stepped from the carriage. He had the cold, probing eyes of a reptile. Brilliant but as distant from his fellow man as his seclusion suggested. His true self was hidden a couple inches beneath skin. Damn it, how he wanted to disagree with Bateman, but....

*I get the same feeling: that man wasn't the Baron.*

"What are you babbling on about?" Georgie asked.

"Thinking aloud," said Paul.

As she saddled close, Paul smelled whiskey on her lips. She'd joined Michael for a drink.

"You don't believe what ol' Michael's sayin', do you? I don't need two loonies about."

"No," Paul admitted, "it's fantastic."

"'Steady,'" she mocked, showing her hand. "Say, my father doesn't disapprove of you, Paul. He says you're a hard worker." Georgie stroked his thigh. "I bet he's right."

*Your father's been murdered*, Paul thought. *I take it back. It's not fantastic at all.* He *was in that box. Your father. He's gone, Georgie.*

"What's the matter?"

"I don't know, but I'm going to see the Baron," Paul said.

*You're crazy—damned crazy.*

"You're daft," Georgie said. "Whatever for?"

"Because Parson Bateman. I think the tyrant is right."

"Right about *what?* About you?"

"Georgie…." The thought died unspoken. It was cruel to suggest the death of her father with no evidence except a gut feeling.

"Don't tell me you're settin' out to impress the old bugger."

"Tell Michael I'm ill," Paul said. He unknotted the apron at his waist.

"Ill? Touched in the head is more like it."

---

THE FOREST INVADED the broken chateau, leaving windows cracked and the sills clogged with vines, leaving once luxurious wallpaper the gray consistency of a wasp nest, leaving a smattering of autumn's dead leaves crumbled in corners. The breath of winter hissed in the fissures. It was humbling to see how quickly nature overtook and undid what the better sort called civilized life. Given time, the wilderness was indiscriminately savage.

Dutch peered at the tall ceiling, thirty feet high in the main hall, and he appreciated the lances of sunlight that kept the interior from being dark as a bruise.

*I'm no child,* he thought. *I'm in control here, ain't I? I brought the goods, after all.*

How easily he had been relieved of those goods.

*The driver,* Dutch thought, *could rip a man asunder.*

The Baron returned. He had shed his coat but not the gloves. His footsteps clacked against tile, echoing between the walls. He was alone.

Dutch wrung his hands.

*I ain't stayin' for dinner and I ain't stayin' for tea*, he thought. *Get on with it.* He decided that, whenever money touched his palm, he'd get on his way, straight out the door and into the snow. *To Hell with these ruins. I'd rather sleep in the cold. To Hell with you, too, Baron, thank you very much.*

The Baron stared into Dutch's eyes. He reached for his breast pocket.

*That's it,* Dutch thought.

Instead of a wallet, the Baron fetched a silver cigarette case. The box opened with a click. He offered one to Dutch.

"I wanna talk price," he said impatiently.

"Let's get you out of the cold first," the Baron said. "You're trembling."

"I don't want no comforts. Did you get a look at it or didn't you?"

"Come," the Baron said, sliding the case into his pocket. He struck a match and lit the cigarette at his lips. Pungent smoke roiled from his nostrils. "We'll talk in the study."

*You better not be giving me a run around, you bastard. You won't be the first man I've cut to pieces.*

The Baron led the way around a Baroque staircase toward a set of double doors steeped in shadow. Hinges groaned as he pulled one of the doors outward. A swath of warm, smoky air escaped. The doorway opened upon a comfortable, ornately furnished study, with a fireplace toward the center and with walls lined in an unbroken stream of leather books. There was a dining table at one of the corners, and atop the table waited various liquors: brandy, cognac, gin, imported bourbon. The driver, his face concealed with cloth, and another, smaller man, his face and hands likewise concealed, stood in front of a bookcase. The smaller man wore a blanket across his shoulders. His bandages were damp.

A disgusting thought occurred to Dutch: *They're bloody lepers. Their skin and meat's falling off the bone.*

"Have a seat," the Baron ordered. His gloved hand motioned at a leather chair.

Dutch sat.

The Baron followed his lead, taking the seat opposite. He stubbed out his cigarette before speaking.

"I've had an opportunity to look over the specimen," he said. The fire crackled over his shoulder.

"Let's say my manners—"

"—Shut up," the Baron said. "Do not speak when I am talking to you."

Dutch chanced a look at the driver and his companion. They stepped closer.

"Sure, friend," he said.

His fist tightened into a ball. He decided to kill the Baron if given a chance. And he'd put the bloody lepers out of their misery while he was at it.

*That's how you become a baron,* he thought. *Why, I'd inherit a castle.*

"I appreciate the condition. It *is* quite old. My study of mummification has—"

"—How much?"

"I have no mark with which to pay you."

Dutch released a shaky breath. "That's not what I wanted to hear, friend."

"I imagine it isn't. There's no beating around the bush with you, is there?"

"I'd say not."

"Fine. I have one way to pay you, but you must be shown rather than told."

"You're foolin' me, aren't you?" Dutch's nerves tightened. The fear he experienced on the bridge crept in.

*I got control here,* he promised.

He mapped the route to the blade in his pocket. Thinking about the Baron's warm blood between his fingers calmed him.

The Baron stood. "I'll show you now."

Dutch pushed himself free of the deep chair.

The Baron walked to a corner of the study. He stood over a blanketed form that Dutch had failed to notice before. There was a man beneath the blanket. Dutch assumed it was another mummy. He said as much.

"No, he hasn't reached that stage yet," the Baron said. "He only died this morning." He knelt and lifted the blanket. "We'll begin the process tonight."

The man was freshly dead, neck swollen, skin choked blue.

"Christopher, fetch our friend, please."

Before Dutch retrieved his knife, the larger of the servants was behind him. His immense strength was clear when he clamped Dutch's arms. Dutch squirmed and struggled and cursed.

"Teach him to be calm, David," the Baron said.

The smaller servant took Dutch's hand into his own.

Dutch spat on gauze wrapping the servant's face. David's watery eyes and purple mouth were free of the bandages. He smelled of rotten flesh and mildew. Consumed with the thought of death, Dutch quit his struggle.

"You're nothing but a worm of a creature," the Baron said. "Will the world miss you?"

David raised Dutch's trembling hand and breathed his cold, fetid breath across the flesh. He gnashed his blackened teeth.

"I'll be calm," Dutch promised.

The Baron produced a syringe from a case on the shelf.

"Would you rather be alive or dead when I embalm you?" he asked. He nodded at the man on the floor. "Unlike you, this man had no choice. That will be your payment."

Dutch, with a singular, animalistic urge in his mind, renewed his struggle against the driver's grip.

David bit into the bones of his fingers, severing the skin.

"Silence him," the Baron ordered.

---

A GREAT DEAL of history lived in Paul's mind as he reached the last house of Karlsbadt, passing the final fence and field. He trawled his memory, dredging up stories.

The last squall of snow had ended an hour before, heading east from town. Along with it, the wind gone. The gray sky broke blue. Despite sunlight, the town and surrounding hills remained arctic. Paul followed the pitted lines of the Baron's carriage. As he began the ascent into the forest, he looked down into the frozen shell of Karlsbadt, recalling the story that troubled him most as a child.

*I'll say it again,* he thought. *You're damned crazy.*

Eyeing the church steeple, which rose higher than any of the rooftops, he thought of Maria. He eyed the tavern and thought of Georgie.

*What's the harm in fetching a look?* he thought.

The old story unfolded atop the other thoughts. He recalled the tale as his father told it.

*There once was a man from Nantucket. He had a… I'll finish the limerick when you're older, son.* Paul smiled. *No, this man was Austrian—that's where the Emperor sat in those days. He arrived a drifter, a traveler. Odd men, travelers, and Karlsbadt isn't friendly to them. I don't know why we have an inn. They told him to be on his way—gave him food and drink and showed him the road. He said he would try the forest for shelter.*

*The Baron's Forest? they asked.*

*Whatever its name. Devil may care, he was.*

*They taunted him with ghost stories and gave him more beer to help him believe. The traveler set off in the dark. He returned to Karlsbadt two days later.*

*What did he say? Paul asked.*

*The Baron brought him down the hill in a casket. He said the forester found the traveler, eaten to a crescent by wolves. The Baron had the people bury the man. No one knew his name.*

*Wolves? There are no wolves here.*

*Exactly, his father said.*

That was all—that, in fact, was the point of the story. There were no wolves. If not wolves, then what ate the traveler? His father didn't conjecture. Paul's imagination was left to wonder, and it still wondered. If there was a moral to the story, it was simple: stay away from the woods or you'll catch your death.

*Boys like to be frightened,* Paul's father told his wife after she scolded him.

Was that all there was to it? A little fear to digest and overcome?

Paul's father, wise man that he was, didn't survive his son's fifteenth birthday. Cancer ate up his body and mind with more ferocity and cruelty than wolves could muster. Parson Bateman had delivered cool, uninspiring words over his grave. He talked about journeys, travelers, and dust becoming dust again. Paul had watched the forest as the reverend spoke.

*My father left me that story for a reason*, Paul thought. *He knew I'd be a man if I overcame it.*

Paul reached the tree line when a voice from behind caused him to halt.

Maria, gasping for breath, said, "Whatever are you doing, Paul?"

*I'm not sure*, he thought.

To Maria, who approached with a pained look on her face, he said, "Your father's correct about the Baron."

"He thinks so. He's rambling on about putting together a group of men. But why on earth does that concern you?"

"How did you know I was here?"

"Georgie stopped by the church and told me you were acting a fool. She was seeing my father about something. Something about her own father. He'd gone this morning and not come back."

*He died*, Paul thought.

He looked upon Maria's delicate beauty. A splotch of red at her cheeks was the only color in her porcelain skin. She had light, green eyes and fanning lashes, and blonde hair that fell over her temples in curls, escaping her shawl. Feeling brave, he pulled her close and kissed her.

"The whole town can see you," she said. Her face was hot with embarrassment and excitement.

"Now you're scandalized," he said. He kissed her again. "Maybe your father will disown you."

Maria pushed his chest, freeing herself.

Paul laughed.

"Wherever you're going, I'm going with you," she said.

Paul reached out his hand. Maria grabbed it. "I'm off to see the Baron," he said.

Together, they walked into the forest, along a sloping road lined with gnarled trees. At length, Paul said, "In honesty, Maria, I don't know if this is something you want to do. I suspect Georgie's father was killed. I suspect the Baron has everything to do with it."

"Why do you say that?"

"That little man in the street earlier. Michael said he had a body in the box he was pulling. Georgie's father disappeared this morning. I don't like the way it adds up."

"If you're right, what do you plan to do about it?"

Paul hadn't thought of that. "I don't know," he admitted. "I want to chance another look at the Baron, I suppose."

"Then you're being a child," Maria said.

The road stretched on for a mile. When the hill leveled, the eaves of the Baron's chateau came into view. Trees obscured the remainder of the home.

"I've never been up here before," Maria said. A touch of awe imbued her voice.

"Neither have I. The stories always—"

"—Stories keep everyone away," Maria finished.

The front gate was unlocked and open, the base of the

iron bars buried in snow. Paul and Maria started along the driveway.

"It's all broken up," Paul said, as the home became clearer. "It's positively gothic." He reached down and grabbed Maria's hand.

"You've had your look," she said. "Now can we go?"

Paul glanced about at the chateau and surrounding forest.

*Maybe the moral of the story is vastly different*, he thought. *My father was as terrified as anyone. Wolves, after all, wear many disguises. Maybe I am being a child.* The same intuition that pushed him out the door became morbid.

*A day of endings.*

"Turn and go, Maria," he said.

She looked at him like he'd lost his mind. "And where do you—"

"Welcome to our home."

The voice that issued from behind a pile of broken furniture by the front gate was garbled, hoarse, and ugly. A man who could have been the Baron's driver, but whom Paul thought much shorter, emerged with an unlit torch in his grip. His face, his hands, his entire body except a slit at his mouth and opening at the eyes was concealed.

"The Baron," he mumbled, "loves travelers."

"We're not travelers," Paul said. "We're from town."

"Oh, well he may like that even better. Or not. I can show you inside."

Paul looked at Maria. "I don't think that will be necessary."

"But I insist," the man said.

As he approached, Paul saw bloodstains on the cotton around his mouth. The man's gait must have been painful because his black gums contorted with every step. He dropped his torch to keep his hands free.

"Go on," he said. "Keep walking."

Paul and Maria walked the driveway with the servant lumbering at their heels. They could imagine little of the terror that waited. Fear and uncertainty kept the couple together—they did not chance separation by running off, by escaping into the wilderness. They would meet the Baron. And they would find that he seduced with kindness. The servants, however, would prove less civil.

Paul, Maria, Georgie's father, and Dutch would be the first in a line of experiments. They would not be the last. The Baron was prepared to reveal his work. Karlsbadt would be a laboratory for this house of murder.

---

IN THE GARDEN OF TREES, he had found a trickling spring. He ordered Christopher and David to kneel and wash deer blood from their faces and hands.

*Impressions*, he said.

Ever since the flesh of his creations began to deteriorate, he worried about impressions. He insisted Christopher and David remain hidden in the garden while he approached the chateau.

*I promise I'll return for you*, he said. *Did I not return for you before?*

He had, they admitted, been true to his word in the past.

*Remove your bandages and let me see you*, he said.

With wet, cumbersome hands, Christopher first, and then David, unraveled the cloth concealing their faces. The sight was diseased and ghastly. Where there was once chalky flesh covering their skulls, now there were slashes of visible bone. Exposed sinew connected the cheek to the lower jaw. The foreheads melted into the brow. Hair had fallen. The eyes were wet as puddles. Lips crumbled into black gums.

Once he figured out a way to halt the deterioration, he would have to graft new faces onto their skulls.

He touched David's bald pate and a strand of Christopher's sparse hair, and he reminded his children the virtue of patience.

David, the more thoughtful of the two, looked ashamed.

*He's becoming existential*, he thought. *I'll have to watch him closely. Of the two, he's more likely to murder himself. Christopher is a simpler creature.*

He stepped from the garden with the air, if not the clothes or perfumed countenance, of a nobleman.

*Regardless, alike men recognize one another*, he thought.

Still, a shallow man would call this highborn man of science a wretched beggar. He was gaunt, hungry, and exhausted, and he wore all this baggage in his eyes.

The chateau that ended the path before him was once resplendent—immense, ornate, Baroque. Now it showed neglect, as though money was scarce. The landed poor, they were called. His own family, if not for the business sense of his grandfather, would have suffered the same decline.

At the front door there was a rope that ran inside to a bell—a contraption rigged without talent. It was a job done in haste.

*These poor people,* he thought.

The bell pealed across the rafters of the main hall. Several minutes later, footsteps approached. A servant pushed open one of the doors. He was a young man with a ruddy earthiness in his features, a dressed-up peasant, a prettified brute.

In a measured tone, he said, "State your business, sir."

He told the boy a story he concocted about a stay in the Balkans, about a prison camp.

*I'm a doctor, a physician.*

He talked about a fire, about political intrigue, and how he needed a warm meal and bed for the night.

The boy, unaccustomed to visitors, rang for his master.

Baron Karlsbadt moved impatiently down the staircase. He was a stocky man who was once fit and strong. He carried the stern, confident manner of an officer. His large mustache shook when he spoke.

"What is all this?" he asked, brandishing a crowbar. "My son and I——" He stopped and looked over the man who could have been a beggar.

"What is your business here?" the Baron asked.

"My name is Frankenstein," he said, "and I'm in need of shelter."

"You can tell your story later," he said. "Right now, I'm in need of an extra man to get this case up the stairs."

Frankenstein stepped into the cool, breezy hall.

The Baron pointed to an oblong box waiting at the base of the steps.

"The three of us should be able to get it upstairs," he said. "My son received a busted arm on the expedition"

"May I ask what's in the box?"

"See that?" the Baron pointed at a black, stenciled word: *Aegyptica.* "The latest for my antiquities collection. It'll be the heart of my cabinet. It's a mummified boy of the Fifteenth Dynasty. Could've been a pharaoh's nephew for all we know. You help us get that box upstairs, and I'll give you all you can eat."

Looking over the box, planks nailed together loosely and hemorrhaging straw, a fantastic idea occurred to Frankenstein. He contemplated the rotting forms of Christopher and David, he thought about his scarred hands that could no longer perform surgery, and he realized the latest road he would travel.

*Mummification,* he thought, *embalming.*

Mummification was the key to halting deterioration. Inspired, forgetting his most recent trauma, he said, "I'm more than happy to assist. Perhaps I can help examine your find. I'm a doctor."

# ABOUT THE AUTHOR

Coy Hall lives in West Virginia, where he splits time as an author of horror and professor of history. His books include *Grimoire of the Four Impostors* (2021), *The Hangman Feeds the Jackal: A Gothic Western* (2022), *The Promise of Plague Wolves* (2023), and *A Seance for Wicked King Death* (2023).

www.coyhall.com

# ACKNOWLEDGMENTS

Collection © 2023 by Coy Hall

NIGHT OF THE RATS' NEST © 2016 by Coy Hall. First appeared in *Hypnos*, Volume 5, Issue 2.

THE SHE-WOLF AND SAINT EDMUND © 2022 by Coy Hall. First appeared in *A 3-B Halloween*.

A PANTHEON OF THIEVES © 2012 by Coy Hall. First appeared in *Abomination Magazine #3*.

HOUR OF THE CAT'S EYE © 2020 by Coy Hall. First appeared in *The Fiends in the Furrows II: More Tales of Folk Horror*.

UNDEAD HELLCATS © 2023 by Coy Hall. Previously unpublished.

THE FROST GIANT: NIGHT OF THE RATS' NEST II © 2023 by Coy Hall. Previously unpublished.

WASP WING © 2016 by Coy Hall. First appeared in *Wax & Wane: A Gathering of Witch Tales*.

SCOURGE OF THE FLESH DEVILS: A TALE OF FRANKENSTEIN © 2016 by Coy Hall. First appeared in *Spawn of the Ripper*.

Made in United States
Orlando, FL
08 May 2023

32915232R00088